Thomas Tomkinson

The Muggletonian Principles Prevailing

Being an answer in full to a scandalous and malicious pamphlet, entitled A

true representation of the absurd and mischievous principles of the sect

called Muggletonians.

Thomas Tomkinson

The Muggletonian Principles Prevailing
Being an answer in full to a scandalous and malicious pamphlet, entitled A true representation of the absurd and mischievous principles of the sect called Muggletonians.

ISBN/EAN: 9783337410186

Printed in Europe, USA, Canada, Australia, Japan

Cover: Foto ©Andreas Hilbeck / pixelio.de

More available books at **www.hansebooks.com**

THE
Muggletonians Principles
PREVAILING:
BEING

An Anſwer in full to a Scandalous and Malitious Pamphlet, Intituled

A

True Repreſentation
OF THE

Abſurd and Miſchevious Principles of the Sect called

MUGGLETONIANS;
WHEREIN

The aforeſaid Principles are Vindicated, and
proved to be infallibly True.

AND

The Author of that Libel, his Scandalous Title and Subject
proved as Falſe to Truth, as Light is to Darkneſs: And
that he knows no more what the true God is, nor what
the right Devil is; nor any true Principle or Foundation of
Faith, for all his great Learning he ſo much boſts of, then
thoſe *Jews* that put the Lord of Life to Death: For learned
and taught Reaſon is but natural, and ſo falls ſhort of the
Glory of God; as will appear in the following Diſcourſe.

---

*Things that are deſpiſed hath God choſen to bring to nought Things
that are,* 1 Cor. 1. 28.

By *T. T.*

Printed in the Year of our Lord God 1695.

The *Epistle* to the sober Reader.

Curtious Reader,

I Have here, in this insuing Treatis, Vindicated the Principles of them People called Muggletonians, *from that Aspersion and Slander that envious Reason hath cast upon it*; I being a Member of that Body, and knowing those Principles to be Truth, having lived in the Knowledg and Practice of them above this Thirty Years.

Now in that Providence should bring thee in, to see this my Answer, and shalt find some things very strange to thy Understanding: And tho, perhaps, thou canst not apprehend it at first View for Truth, yet if thou canst preserve thyself from dispising it, thou dost well to thy own Soul.

Therefore keep thyself from Judging, if thou wilt live in Peace, because that none can judg of *Spiritual Things* but Spiritual Men: And know this, that the un-judging Man is easy, and may afterwards come to Believe, being in the time of a Commission, and so with the Five wise Virgins bring Oyle in their Lamps, before the Dore be shut, or Death aproach. 1 Cor. 2. 15.

Matt. 25. 4.

But to Contend against Truth held forth by a Commission from Heaven, is an evident Sgn of Rejection, for it will prove a Sin against the Holyghost : *Therefore I advise thee but to take care of these Two Things ;* the one, Not to break the Law; *the other,* Not to despise Prophefy, *because they are both* Damnable: *And more People are Damned for breaking the Law than any other Sin, for the Sin against the Holyghost is not committed in every Age, but only in the time of a Commission ; so that more People have committed that Sin within this Forty four Years then hath done of Thirteen Hundred and Fifty Years*
before:

[4]

before: So that *thefe* Two *things are to be fhun'd, the laft*

Matc. 12. 32.
Rom. 6. ult.
1 Cor. 6. 11.
Ephe. 2. 1.

moft efpecially, becaufe there is no Sacrifife for that Sin, but the other is Pardonable in the time of a Commiffion, by having Faith in the Doctrin thereof, and living free from the Breach of the Law after, as to the Act. This *is the Benefit of a true* Miniftry, *but no true* Miniftry, *no true* Converfion *from the Act of Sin: But the* Elect

Jer. 23. 32.

are preferved from the Act of Sin, and kept in innocency of Life, *at fuch* Times, *and in fuch* Places *as Truth is not known by their generated Faith, which leads them to*

Mich. 6. 8.

that Threefold Precept of the Prophet Micha. 1ft. To do Juftice, 2dly. To loue Mercy, *and* 3dly. To walk humbly with God: *This is the Subftance of pure and undefiled Religion:* Stand faft here, and be Happy.

So that from what thou findeft here written, thou upon fight thereof muft examine thy own Heart, and fee how it ftands in this Cafe; if thou canft prove thy Election by Faith in the true God, now he is made manifeft, it is well for thee, and the Benifit will be thine; but if thou canft not believe it, yet if thou difpifeft it not, thou art not againft us, nor againft thy own Soul, neither are we againft thee, be of what Religion or Opinion thou wilt; but fhall leave thee as the Two Seeds fhall find thee at the laft Day.

And fo wifhing well to all fober Men, but more efpecially, to fuch as are not offended with thefe plain Truths touching the Lord Jefus Chrift being that moft High and Mighty God, and Everlafting Father, fo abundantly exalted through the Scriptures of Truth, as is now explained and fully declared, by the Third and Laft fpiritual Commiffion, which was to finifh that facred Miftery of God's becoming Flefh; and now it is finifhed, if thou canft Believe: And he that hath Ears to hear, let him hear.

FAREWEL.

THE

THE
MUGGLETONIANS
PRINCIPLES
PREVAILING.

CHAP. I.

THe Church of God was never without oppofition; nor Truth without Hatred; for in
that there are two Seeds, there muft be a
War entroduced, becaufe the Seeds are in oppofition
to each other, being from two feveral Roots, Faith
and Reafon, Light and Darknefs, God and Devil;
fo that the Seed of the Woman and the Seed of the
Serpent will hould continually Enmity.

Now you that have Accufed the *Muggletonians*
Principles for *Impioufe,* and *Mifchevious,* let us come
to the *Tryal* of it, with you and of you, and fee how
you durft be fo bold, as to make fo falfe a Reprefentation of the *Muggletonians Principles;* that you
fhould Intitle your *Diabolical Pamphlet* by the name
of a *True Reprefentation* of the *Abfurd* and *Mifchevious*
Principles, of the *Sect* called *Muggletonians.*

If you the *Writer* thereof, had caft them Afperfions
upon our Perfons, and not upon our Principles, we
would have borne it with filence, but in that you
B   have

have judged our Faith to be Blafphemous and Mifchevious, which we have received from the Bounty and Love of God; therefore in difpifing and condemning it, you difpife and condemn our God; fo in this Cafe we muft refift you, and ftand forth for the defence of our Faith.

And altho it fhould be where Satans Seat is, yet we will not let go our Inheritance, for our Inheritance lies in the Belief of our Principles, wherein we have the Charter of Heaven fealed to us; therefore we will not only vindicate thofe our Principles, which you fo wickedly Reprefent, but will alfo, through Grace, feal to them with our Blood, if your Law can do it, and we be called thereunto.

For we are able to maintain thofe Principles for Truth; therefore let us now come to the Tryal of Truth, and let us fet our Principles each againft the other; and them, whofe Faith and Wifdom is greateft, let them hold the other under in Bondage for ever.

Sir, You are come forth to Curfe a quiet and ftill People, who meddle not with your Affairs, nor Magiftrates Affairs: We lift not up our Hand, nor make ufe of a Sword of Steel to flay any Man: We defraud no Man, we wrong no Man; neither are we for thrufting you out of your Earthly Poffeffions; no, not out of your Pulpits or Parifh-Livings; we will have none of them: But on the contrary, we are Obedient unto all the Civil Laws of the Land, and give to every Man the Refpect due unto him.

All therefore that we defire of you is, That we may pafs peacibly through your Country towards our Inheritance; but you are not willing that we fhould, no more than *Edom* was with *Iffrael*; but have prefumed to ftop our Courfe, by judging and condeming

Numb. 20.

ing

ing our Faith: Now if our Faith be true, as we know it is, then you have given Judgment againſt your ſelf; you were not aware of that Caution of our Saviours Saying, *Judg not, and thou ſhalt not be Judged;* Matt. 7. 1. Now in that we know that our Faith is of God, and is Truth, therefore is it of Power to reign over that which judgeth it.

But if we might come to Reaſon together, then I would demand of you, wherefore you did ſend our your judging Pamphlet againſt us, and would not ſubſcribe your Name to it? Were you afraid of holding Tryal with us, for fear you ſhould be worſted by us, as others have been heretofore; and ſo were for working Miſchief privately, and yet ly *in Cognito*, thinking, belike, that Faiths Power could not find you out, to give you an Anſwer; otherwiſe how could you find a Name to your Book, and a Name to the People you wrote againſt, but have found never a Name for your ſelf, but have left it to us to find a Name for you, which according to holy Writ is *Elima* a Corrupter, a Acts 13. 10. ſworn Enemy to Truth, and the Accuſer of the Brethren; being of a worthy Deſcent, Succeſſor to *Simon Magus*; being newly crept out of the Colledg of Prieſts, which came out of the Mouth of the Falſe Rev. 16. 13. Prophet; ſuch a one as *Amaziah* the Prieſt of *Beth-el,* Amos 7. 12. who could not abide a poor Prophet, a Herds-Man, that he ſhould once ſpeak near the King's Chappel, becauſe it was the King's Court, in which Learned *Amaziah* was the Doctor and Chaplain.

Thus have you delt with theſe Prophets of the Lord; and for fear that this poor Prophets Doctrin (which you, like *Amaziah*, call Miſchevious) ſhould take any Epheƈt amongſt the People: From hence you have ſecretly ſpred this your Pamphlet unto

your

your Brethren, the Priefts, Hands, all the Nation o-
ver; and have endeavoured to make our Principles as
Contemptable and Odious as poffibly you could, in
order to make them feem the more Rediculous; and
this your Book muft be as a Pattern for them to frame
their Arguments by; and thofe their Arguments muft
be as Bulworks of Defence to them, and as Bullets
fhot againft us.

Efther. 3. 8. *Sir,* You have acted in the very fame way as *Ha-*
man did againft *Ifrael,* faying in this manner to the
King, *There is a certain malitious and mifchevious Peo-*
ple fcattered abroad amongft the People in all places, and
their Laws are differing from all People; neither keep they
the King's [Church-Laws] *therefore it is not for the*
King's profit to fuffer them; let them be deftroyed; for
their Principles *are mifchevious.*

Now I being a Member of this difpifed People, feeing your Spite and Malice againft us (who have broke
no Law) am from hence moved to return an Anfwer,
and this my Reply fhall not fpare you, altho I am given to underftand, That you are a Doctor of the National Church, for God and Faith is no refpecter of
Perfons in fuch a Cafe; Therefore this my Reply fhall
perfue you until it overtake you; and when it hath
overtaken you, it fhall faften a Witnefs in your Confcience, that you have been a Fighter againft God,
his Prophets and People, and againft the Sacred Scriptures; and a falfe Reprefenter of the *Muggletonian's* Principles, and I fhall not be long in proving the fame: For,

In the Preface of your Book you fay, That *John*
Reeve was, by Profeffion, a Baker; which Saying of
yours is utterly Falfe: So here you haue forfited your
Title-Page, which inftead of a true Reprefentation is
a falfe one.

But

But you bring him in as a Baker, to make him the more Contemptible with the Learned; but if he had, would that have made him more uncapable of being God's laſt Meſſenger, I tro not, no more than it did *Amos,* who was but a Herds-Man as aforeſaid.

For this is evident, that the Saints have found in all Ages, that the Learned have ever ſtood up as an Enemy and Judg of ſpiritual Truth; as will more appear in the ſequel of my Diſcourſe: But to proceed to

The Accuſation againſt us.

In your Preface you call us, *poor deluded Souls, and by the Name of a contemptible and pernicious Sect*; and blaſphemiouſly affirm, *that it is made up of* Impiety, Nonſence, *and* Abſurdities; *and that we have not ſo much as the Shadow of Reaſon to ſupport us:* From hence, ſay you, *we will not ſubmit to the Tryal of it, being uncapable of Argument, and that you wrote not that your Treatiſe for our Sakes, that have not Reaſon and Argument* (as you ſay) *to anſwer you; but for the Sakes and Satisfaction of the World, and of the Learned, who are capable* (ſay you) *to bear Reaſon and Argument.*

CHAP. II.

ANSWER.

AS to them Judging and Condemning Cenſures againſt us, ſhall be anſwered *Chap.* 15. And as to your Reaſon and Argument, you ſo much boſt of, I am willing to allow it its Prerogative, and
give

Deut. 1. 13
Acts 26. 3.
& 18. 14, 15.
give it its due of having Government as to all Terreſtial Affairs.

But wherefore ſhould it enter upon God's Prerogative, ſo as to take upon it to judg divine Things
Luke 20. 14. that are Eternal, by its unclean ſerpentine Reaſon.

Matt. 11. 25.
But to ſuch as are learned in Faith's School doth know, that he that doth Miniſter ſpiritual Things, is to lay Reaſon and Argument by, as to the finding out of any heavenly Secrets by the moſt perſingſt Reaſon that is.

James 3. 15.
For Reaſon is not Heaven-born, and ſo is but Natural; and it is the natural or moral Law that enlightens it; but Faith being of another Nature, which
Pſal. 19. 7.
John 1. 4.
is Spiritual, and ſo the Law of Faith ſerves to quicken and enlighten Faith; and when it is enlightened, then ſhe Rules as Miſtreſs over Reaſon.

Therefore, though the Kingdoms of this World lys in Reaſon, yet the Kingdom of Chriſt lys in Faith,
John 18. 36.
Luke 17. 21.
2 Cor. 1. 12.
which ever appears ſimple, and yet it is this poor deſpiſed Seed that receives the Goſpel; its the Simple
Luke 1. 53.
& 6. 25
and the Fooliſh that catch Heaven: The Poor are filled with the Subſtance of ſpiritual Truth, when as the Rich in Reaſon, Notion, and Argument, are ſent empty away.

Therefore away with your Arguments where Faith
Matt. 4. 18.
Amos 1. 1.
Acts 18. 3.
Coll. 2. 8.
is ſought, there the *Fiſher*, the *Herds-man*, the *Tentmaker*; Ai, and he that you call the *Baker*, rather than the *Philoſopher*, are to be truſted.

Do you teach the World by your Reaſon and Argument, as you ſay; this manifeſts that you and your Brethren are the Worlds Miniſters, and the World hears you; and hence it is that you appeal to
1 John 4. 5.
John 7. 7.
the World, for the World will Love its own.

Here

Here now you appear to be a right Legolift, in imi- Deut: 27.
tation of the *Levits* of old; for that Priefthood was Judg: 17. 10;
to teach Reafon, the Moral Law for its reafonable
Service, that it fhould not *Murder, Commit Adultery,
Steal,* or *bare falfe Witnefs,* which Reafon is fubject
to do.

But all the Prophets fpiritual Declarations belong- Pfal. 119. 100.
ed to the Elect Seed of Faith, and was fpoken into
that innocent Nature that cannot do Evil, and that
in order to a further degree of Knowledg, Love and
Obedience.

Wherefore then, if by your Teaching you can
keep your Difciples in Sobriety and the Bounds of
Reafon, this is a Virtue, and brings with it the
Temporal Blefling promifed that Seed; but if fo it be, Deut. 28. 2,3,
that your Reafon will feek Lordfhip, and would be a 4, 5, 60
Judg and Controwler of Faith, it is nothing lefs than John 19. 7.
a Devil, and will be damn'd to Eternity. Mat. 18. 6.

And herein appears your Blindnefs, notwithftanding your earthly Wifdom, becaufe by it you cannot
diftinguifh betwixt the Two Seeds of Faith and Rea- Ezek. 34. 17.
fon, or the Law and the Gofpel. But to proceed, 1 John 1. 17.
and come to the Matter in Queftion.

Would you Priefts have us be tryed by your Arguments? Then you are like to have the Caufe, if
you muft be your own Judges, like the *Jews* by our
Saviour, his Prophets and Apoftles.

But this we prefume to tell you, that your Reafon,
being but Natural, therefore it cannot try fpiritual 1 Cor. 2. 13.
Truth, but our Faith can try your Arguments, and it 1 John 4. 1.
can take up Reafon as a Servant, to argue with you Rom. 2 2.
in the Balance of your own Reafon, the Angels Na- Acts 17. 2.
ture fallen; neverthelefs we can no more agree than & 24, 25.
the Prophet *Jeremiah* and thofe National falfe Priefts
did in the like Difpute. Be-

·Becaufe Faith, when it takes up Reafon, it takes it up, not to expound and open the Sence of Scripture Sayings, but as a Servant, to Illuftrate that Revealed Word by Argument, for the further Confounding of that unclean domineering Reafon that doth oppofe its fpiritual Sence.

But on the contrary, when learned Reafon takes up Words of Faith, it expounds it by the Imagination of Reafon, in refpect its Reafon is Lord in its Soul, and fo turns Truth into a Ly; and the Elogancy of its Speech muft form the Subftance of the Matter, and then War is proclaimed againft the Truth, and fo Truth muft be trod under Foot.

Thus did the falfe Priefts deal by *Jeremiah, Come,* fay they, *let us devife Devifes againft him, and let us deftroy the Tree with its Fruit, and let us cut him off that his Name may be no more Remembred:* That is, let us deftroy his Perfon, which is the Tree; and let us deftroy its Fruit, that is, his Doctrin or Declarations, for he is in bringing in another Priefthood, therefore Report and we will Report; let us frame our Arguments againft him, for he faith, *That they that handle the Law know not God,* when as it is written, *That the Law fhall not perifh from the Priefts, nor Counfel from the Wife.*

Mifreprefenting Doctor, are not your Arguments anfwerable to theirs, even to a Hair: Therefore as true Wifdom was departed from them, fo it is now from you, and from all thofe National pretended Gofpel-Minifters, tho you boft as they did; yet have you nothing but an empty Title, not fo much as a grain of fpiritual Senfe appeareth; but as it was their Blindnefs, fo it is yours, who underftand not, that the fpiritual Law of Faith will never depart from that

fpiritual

Marginal references:

Rom. 1. 25.
Revel. 3. 9.

1 Cor. 1. 20.
Revel. 11. 2.

Jer. 11. 19.

Jer. 18 18.
& 20. 10.
&. 2. 8.
Mal. 2. 7.

Spiritual Prieſt, the true Chriſtrian, but his Lips ſhall Ezek. 7. 26, ever preſerve true Knowledg: And this Prieſthood will 1 Pet. never terminate, but will be with them to the end of the World.

For after Faith is enlightened by a Commiſſion from Heaven, then it needs no other Teacher, but that Uncti- 1 John 2 27 on which it hath received; for the Spritit of Faith is Chriſt's Vicar.

But your outward viſible Worſhips that are taken up from former Commiſſions, they are ended, and the ſpirit of God is gone out of them; but this will bring a Box upon my Cheeks, by you Non-Commiſſionated Miniſter, as your Predeceſſor did to *Micaiah* the Prophet, with a, 1 Kings 22. 24. *Which way went the ſpirit of God from me to thee.*

But as the Law of Faith, which we have known and Iſa. 59. 21. received, will never depart from us, ſo we need not to Heb. 10. 38. your aſſumed counterfit Prieſthood, but live by our own generated Faith now awakened, or eluminated, Epheſ. 5. 14. by the Doctrin of this Commiſſion of the ſpirit; for we have no new Faith given, but the old awakened, as aforeſaid; for Faith was but once given, and every Com- 2 Pet. 5. 18. miſſionated Prophet, Meſſenger, or Miniſter of God, Ads a further Light and Knowledg to it.

So that now, through Grace, we have attained to a more principal Degree of Knowledg of the true God, and the right Devil, than others had before us; ſo that from hence, we are not wanting in Wiſdom to anſwer your ſtrongeſt Arguments your Reaſon can deviſe, Iſa. 41. 21.

Therefore muſter up your Army, raiſe all your Forſes, from all parts, and from all your Prieſts that you have diſtributed your Books to; yet ſhall you never be able to diſprove by your Subtilty, quell by your Power, or Iſa. 26 1. ſubdue by your Force, the *Muggletonian's* Principles, becauſe Salvation, and nothing leſs is their aſſured Walls and Bulworks.　　　　C　　　　But

But to your following Arguments,
to Anſwer by truth of Scripture.

The Accuſation againſt

In Page the Firſt, you make your B
Two *Queries.* *Firſt,* Whether *John Reev*
Muggleton, are ſent of God. *Secondly,* V
the Witneſſes ſpoken of in the 11th. of

To your *Firſt Querie* ; You have larg
veral of their Saings, which you ſay, tl
true Characters, and Evidences of the
Now, after your Ramble in Page the 4th
dence is, That *John Reeve* ſaith, *That God*
Mornings together : And ſay you, *Muggl.*
is God's ſpeaking plain Words, to the hear
Ear, as well as the inward Soul, that dot
Commiſſioner.

This Evidence, ſay you, *is of no value* ;
I cannot tell, whether it be a true Voice, o
ing Voice, ſuch a one as John Reeve *ſaid*
bins : *It is,* ſay you, *but their ſay ſo.*
conclude ſaing ; *For let their Voice be nev*
alone, and without the viſible Evidence of a
it is of no value: As alſo, you ſay, *it muſt t*
ture ; without which you make it of nc

CHAP. III.

ANSWER.

1. THis your way is to overthrow all Prophefy: You will tie God to worke Miracles, or you will not belive him : Either God muft do as you will have him, or he muft not be God. *Numb. 1. 19. 2 Pet. 1. 19. 1 Thef. 5. 20.*

It is no wonder that you cannot diftinguifh between a true Voice and a falfe; becaufe God never chofe you by Voice, nor never will. But how fhould you believe a vocal Voice, when as your God has never a Tongue : You have made it here plainly appear, that you are of the fame Spirit of thofe murthering *Jews* who bid Chrift, *come down from the Crofs and they would belive in him.* True *Matt. 27. 42.* Doctrin, without Miracles, is to you moft deteftable.

2. Again, was not all true Prophets chofen by voice of Words ; neverthelefs the Seed of the Serpent could never believe them, neither could the Priefts or Rulers ever abide them; and there was few of them but what was either Perfecuted or put to Death, by the Magiftrates and their National Priefts: There was 450.falfe Prophets, muftred up againft Too or Three true Prophets, as Elijah and *Micaiah* ; and one of them muft ftrike *Micaiah* one the Cheek ; as aforefaid, and this Prieft and *Ahab's* Son flung him down to bracke his Neck. *Ifa. 6. 8. & 54. 1. Jer. 15. 10. 1 Kings 18. 22.*

But *Elijah*, the Reprefentor of God's Perfon, by Word of Power flew them all, as a Tipe of the Deftruction of all falfe Prophets, and falfe Priefts, at the end of the World : Such a Miracle you want. *Zeph. 1. 4.*

When *Ifaiah* Prophefied of his God's becoming Flefh, not one would believe him, neither Prieft nor People : *Ifaiah 55. 1.*

C 2　　　　　　　　　　　Therefore,

Therefore, faid he, *Lord, who hath believed our Re-*
1 Kings 19. *port;* and *Elijah* faid, *That all were gon after* Baall. Nor
regarded Truth, for that was ever hated; *I hate him,* faid
1 Kings 22 8. *Ahab, for he never faid Good of me, but Evil;* It's now as
it was then, unlefs we could bring Fire from Heaven, as
Elijah did, there can be no Belief; and it muft be to deftroy them; it might Convince them, but it would ne-
rial. 78. 52. ver Convert them.

If Miracales were wrought now, what would it avail
to this bloody unbeliveing World; they would but fay as
Matt. 12. 24. the *Jews* faid of Chrift, *That they were don by the Devil.*

But what faid *Paul,* Toungues and Miracles are but
for a Signe, not to them that believe, but to them that
1 Cor. 14. 22. believe not; but Prophefy ferveth for them that be-
John 10. 41. lieve only : *John* the *Baptift,* a great Prophet, and yet
did no Miracle.

Thus you call in queftion the glorious Truths of God,
under pretence of *John Reeves's* Weaknefs, as to outward
Miracles, that you might believe, when as his Commiffion is all fpiritual.

Now the Seed of Faith believes not, becaufe of the
Miracles wrought, by the Lord or his Prophets; but in
that they were of the Election, and fore-ordain'd to
believe, for the faving of the Soul ; and as the Chriftian Dove waits for a Sign within him, or from behind
Isa. 30. 21. Reafon, for a Word faying, *This is the Way, walk in it:*
Even fo, on the contrary, the carnal Serpent, he re-
quires a natural Sign before his Reafon, that may be
feen with his outward Eye, to make him believe fpiritual Truths; and therefore Reafon Cries, faying,
*Where are your Miracles, and where is your Scripture Evi-
dence to prove it:* Prove by Scripture.

Now if this Witnefs fhould write nothing but what
is exactly fet down in Scripture, then fhould they
write

write nothing at all: But always true Prophefy hath
fomthing new to deliver. Jer. 31. 22.
 Again, Did the Prophets and Apoftles write, by
Imitation, or Study, or by Infpiration only ; they might Matt. 15. 32.
allude fomtimes to the Prophets Words for Convincing 2 Pet. 1. 21.
of Gainfayers.
 Furthermore, the Scriptures in themfelves are Words
of pure Truth, to all that fpiritually differn them; and
that is, fuch as have the Life and Power of them in
their own Souls; but they that have not the inner Life John 6. 53.
and Meaning thereof, they ftudy the outward Letter by
their Reafon, to find the Life and Meaning thereof, and
then,this their Imagination,the Child of ftudy, trumpits Obed. 6. 8.
out it's own Conceptions upon it. John 7 52.
 This is the work and way of all the feven Anty Churches of *Europe*, every one of them endeavouring to prove
their Miniftry by the Letter of the Scripture, or by the
Light within them ; but never a one from the glorious
Voice of the everliving God without them : And from
hence, though they Judg and Condemn each other for
falfe,whilft they are all falfe, yet can they agree to Fight
aginft God and his true Prophets, by the Letter of the
Scripture.
 And you keep thefe Chefts and Boxes of prefious
things, but the Jewels and Treafure is quite gon, and
is a Stranger to you; you know it not, but do Defpite
unto it, and put your own Imaginations into the Letter, 2 Pet. 2. 18.
and fo turn and wind it about like a Nofe of Wax, and verfe 4
make it fpeak for your Honour and Riches. Oh! how Jude 15. 16.
profitable hath this Letter of the Scriptures been to
Reprobate Preachers.
 Wherefore then, we who are called *Muggletonians*,
in fcorn do boldly affirm, That though you have got the
Letter of the Scriptures, and run away with it, as a
Dogg

Dogg doth with a Bone, yet none of its fpiritual Declarations were ever written for your Inftruction, but for
the Inftruction of the Seed of Faith: For the Law only
belongs to you, and it may make you wife, but not
unto Salvation; that's the Property of the Gofpel to
the Seed of Faith, the Seed of the Lord's own Body; for
it is the Man of God that is made Wife unto Salvation;
fo that he muft be a Man of God, and have Faith in
thofe Scriptures, before he can be Wife unto Salvation,
becaufe they are given by Infpiration of the holy Spirit,
and no Man can know them but by the fame Spirit as
thofe had that wrote them.

Thefe things confidered, how then is it poffible that you
fhould apply Scripture to purpofe, when your Wifdom
is not Infpiration, but Education; what will your Form
do to you without the Power: If you have the Words of
God, and not that Word which is God, what good will
your Word do you.

What Commiffion have you to preach to the People;
Chrift tells you that you are but Thieves and Robbers
climbing up to Heaven by Ordinances of your own, and
your own ftollen Doctrine; for you fteal the Words
from your Neighbour, the Seed of Faith, and then Cry,
Thus faith the Lord.

What do you bring as an Offering, but what you
have ftolen from others; do you delver anything but
Trafcriptions and Hiftorical Notions, the Repetitions
of the Letter of the Scriptures. and the Sentences of
the antient Fathers; there is the Line you boaft in, fo
that you do no more, in ephect, but rob the Dead to
cloath the Living: For have you fo muth as openedthe
Meaning of one Text of Scripture in all your blind
Pamphlet; you have named the Words, and then left
them to Anfwer for them felves, as I fhall fhew hereafter.   Again,

Rom. 15. 4.
Deut. 4. 6.
Jer. 9. 2.

2 Tim. 2. 15.

1 Cor. 4. 20.

John 10. 1.

2 Cor. 10. 16.

Again, you further Object againſt their Doctrin of Infalibility, in that they ſay, *They write by an unerring Spirit*: Now, ſay you, *an Infalible Spirit implys the higheſt Certainty*: But, ſay you, *his Book is Inconſiſtant with it ſelf;* for *Muggleton* ſaith, *I am perſwaded in my ſpirit, and I do rather belive that there were Seven Hundred Thouſands, than Seven Thouſands, though the Revelation of* John *doth* Revel. 11. 13. *but expreſs it but Seven Thouſands*: Now, ſay you, *to be perſwaded, and to belive a Thing to be ſo, are Inconſiſtant to Infalibility;* for that admits no leſs than I am ſure of it, ſay you.

CHAP. IV.

ANSWER.

THE Prophets did both of them write, by an infallible and un-erring Spirit, the Doctrine of themSix Principles, the Knowledg of which, Salvation doth John 17 3 depend upon; but as to ſome perticular Points that are beſides the Foundation, there is not that Neſſeſſity to be ſo poſitive. But as to the Eſſential Points of Faith, they were written by an un-erring Spirit, and are infallibly True; and againſt Men and Angels they affirm it, and we as truly believe it, to the great Peace and Satisfaction of our Minds : For what is it that can ſatisfy the Mind of Man but Truth, having the Seal of Life in it, as every true Miniſter of God hath.

For every true Miniſter of God hath Power to ſet Life and Death before Men and can ſay, *Now is fulfilled* Matt. 18. 18. *ſuch and ſuch Things* : Alſo he that is ſent of God, 1 Cor. 2. 11. knoweth the Things of God, and he that believeth in ſuch a One, knoweth the Things of God likewiſe.

But

But how can you judge of Infalibility; that do not own your felf Infalible, but Falible? What is Falible but a Lye, and muft a Lye be the Judge of Truth? He that knoweth the Mind of the Lord, he may Inftruct from the Lord; but he that hath not the Infalible Spirit, doth from his lying Spirit prefcribe Rules to God, and would be God's Counfellor.

1 Cor. 2. 15.
Verfe 16.

Now muft fuch ignorant, carnal, flefhly Men as thefe Judge Infalibility, that have, nor own no other Spirit but what is Falible: But to come to the Point and Charge againft *Lodowick Muggleton.*

For although the Prophets and Apoftles were Infalible, as to all effential points of Faith; yet as to other things that were circumftantial, and not fo effential, in fuch things Prophets and Apoftles may differ about them in their Experience and Judgment.

Gal. 2. 11.

Thus *Paul* withftood *Peter*, and Reproved him; and though *Paul* there gainfaid *Peter*, yet in fome other things *Paul* himfelf was not pofitive: As for Inftance, *Paul* treating on Marriage, he fpeaks as the Prophet *Muggleton* doth here, and tells the Believers, *That it was his Judment, That it were better for them not to Marry*: And further adds *That he* [thinks,] *That this his Judment is right, and that it was from the Spirit of God.*

1 Cor. 7. 6.

Vrfe 39. 40.

Now, I prefume, (by what you have faid of thefe) that had you been living then, and had heard of *Paul*'s talking of having the Infalible Spirit of God, you would prefently have judged him a falfe Apoftle, notwithftanding the Miracles he had done; and that he had contradicted himfelf; and that his [*thinking*] was inconfiftant to his Infalibility, and fo was not to be Believed.

Again, if you had heard that *Paul* Circumcifed *Timothy*, and yet neverthelefs told the *Galatians*, *That if they were Circumcifed they could not be Saved*. I fay, had you been

Acts 16. 3.
Gal. 5. 2.

been in thofe Days, Would not you have faid, *That* Paul *had Contradicted himfelf, and the Scriptures both?* and would not you alfo have judged the Four Evangelifts to have Contradicted one another in fe- ^{Matt. 28. 2.} veral places; for as you Judg and Condemn thefe,fo you ^{Luke 24. 2.} would have Judged them, for thefe were fent by Jefus Chrift, and *Paul* was fent by no other God.

Again, in *Page 9.* you quote *John Reeve,* faying, that he faith, *That he is Indued with a divine Gift, to write a* Volom *as large as the Bible; and as pure a Language as that is, without looking into any Book, or having any real Contradiction in it.* Upou thefe Words you make the Reflection fallowing.

Your Accufation runs thus, faying.

That if the purity of the Language be a Sign of Truth. *Then,* fay you, *I am fure it is far from being either True or Infallible.* For, faid you, *they do not write true* Englifh, *nor good Sence;*as likewife, *it often fails in the propriety of Words, in Concord; and Connexion; being without Method, Purity, or Elogancy,* &c.

———— ———— ———— — —— —— ———

D   C H A P.

CHAP. V.

ANSWER.

SIR, in Anfwer to this, The truly Wife do know, that God's Meffengers never regard finenefs of Speech, but foundnefs of Matter: Not fo much the Original of Words as the Original of Things, even fuch as they, are moved too by the Holy Ghoft; and not fuch Language as you are moved too by your Educated Spirit of Reafon; which is the Angels nature Fallen: But in that, you have no where contradicted our Principle, which fhews what the Perfon and Nature of Angels are; therefore there is no Occafion given here to Difpute it; but to Return to the matter aforefaid.

Spiritual Truth, or Gofpel Life, was ever plain, and was never delivered with new quined or high-flown Words of Man's Wifdom. This made an old learned Philofophical Bifhop Judge fo hard by the *Revelation* by *John*, not thinking it *John's*, becaufe of the Rudenefs of the ftile: *For,* faid he, *I fee his Greek not exactly uttered, the Dialect and Phrafe not obferved: I find him,* faid this Bifhop, *ufing barbarous Phrafes.*

And *Paul* was called *a clouter of Skins,* a *Cobler* by the Philofophers, and *a Man of no Breeding:* And he acknowledged himfelf but rude in Speech, though not in true Wifdom; but he had taken fome Learning up at the Foot of *Gamalial,* but he laid it down there again, as foon as the Spirit of Faith became his Teacher: All his Wifdom that he now valued, was the Knowledge of Chrift Crucified, and, Rifen again;

· Cor. 2. 1.

Dionifius.

again; which his former Wifdom could not know, Acts 22. 3. but on the contrary, was the Perfecutor of him.

Again, Spiritual Truth, or Faith, was ever brought in Naked and Simple, and in poor Array: But Falfhood doth ever indeavor to Attire herfelf in all her Bravery. *Thefe Rafcals*, faid the *Pharifes*, *are Accurfed*, *they know not the Law*: But faid *Paul*, *That Learning of theirs will conæto nought* 1 Cor. 12. 8.

But as for Truth, That guides to Heaven; it needs no Glofs to make it feem better then it is, for it hath Light enough in it felf, to fhew it the way to Heaven. John 1. 4.

The Scriptures were written in as homely a ftile as *Reeve*'s and *Muggleton's* were; only wife Men in Reafon, have put them into a better Form, and now boaft of their litteral Accutenefs, whilft they are out of all fpiritual Power; and it muft be fo, for he that hath learned nothing of Truth, muft Teach by an Eloquent Tongue of empty Words only. 1 Cor. 13. 1.

For Sophifters, who want fubftance of Truth, muft ufe their Sophiftry, to corrupt Truth, and adulterate the true Sence, and then cover their own Errors with Paint.

And thus have you done. in this Libel of yours; for in Page 18. you affirm, That *John Reeve* doth fay, (pretending to quote his Words) *That the Subftances of Earth and Water were from all Elements* : When as *John Reeve*'s Words were in that place, *That the Subftance of Earth and Water was from all Eternity.*

Thus you turn their good Sence into Nonfence, and fo bely them; for by this your way of clowding their Words you would darken the Sence, and make them appear the more Rediculous; and to prevent a further Difpute in that Subject, *of the Subftance of Earth*

D 2. *and*

and Water being made of nothing, which you were not
able to maintain; and though you fay, *you would confute
that Principle,* yet paffed it by, and would fay no more
of it : And fo you let it drop.

Now, as to your Elogancy of Speech; your
Tongues and Languages you boﬅ fo much of (and
you have need of it to paint your Errors, as aforesaid) we will leave this all to you *Babal* Builders, as
acquired by your Study and Learning; it being
your Trade, which teacheth your Reafon to play upon the Letter of the Scripture as upon a Harp, being
very mellodious to the outward Ear : And by thefe
means you (*Arts-Maﬅers*) grow Rich and Honoura-
ble, according to your skilful Merchandiﬁng of the
Letter of the Scripture, and Antient Fathers and
Philofophers : Thefe muﬅ all be made to agree together, for the Scripture muﬅ either make good Philofophy, or elfe Philofophy muﬅ be brought to make
good the Scripture; and in your wife handling of
this, you grow Rich; fome *Hundreds,* fome *Thoufands*
a Year, equalling the gr at Men of the Earth; and
as to others of your Brethren, though they be more
inferior, yet muﬅ they be called Maﬅers, although
they be but Servants; yet will they be well paid,
for no Penny, no Paternoﬅer.

So having found you all in the way of *Balam,* to
Blefs and Curfe for Mony, which is your Souls chief
Delight, there I leave you to go on in your Trade,
and receive your Wages of Men here, and of God
hereafter, whom you pretend to ferve; then will
you have a full Reward.

A further Accufation againﬅ this Witnefs you
have, for affirming *the Power of Sealing Men up unto
Eternal Life and Death, as they Receive or Difpife*
their

marginal notes:
R. vel. 18, 1.
Revel. 18. 7.
Mr. 23. 7.
Mica. 3. 11.
John 10. 13.
Jude 11.
Phil. 3. 19.
Matt. 6. 5. &
7. 23

their Doctrin: This you deny, that any Man ever had this Power: Saying, *That it is quite contrary to the Scripture, and the Temper of the Gospel, which is Love ;* and then bid us prove it by Scripture.

C H A P. VI.

A N S W E R.

I T is confessed by us, that the Temper of the Gospel is *Love;* but then that Gospel and Eternal Love is but to the Seed of the Lords own Body, and it must needs be so, because that Grace is written in Faiths Nature; and though that Seed did fall in *Adam,* yet the Gospel came to seek and to save that which was lost and fell in *Adam;* for the *Serpent's* Seed never fell in *Adam,* nor never knew themselves lost. So the Gospel belongs not to them, but according to their Obedience to their own Law, so they have the Blessing of the Law, *That the Rain may Rain, and the Sun may Shine, and the Earth bring forth her Increase, with long Life and Health:* And thus *Christ,* which is the Gospel, shewed his Love to that Seed, when he wept over *Jerusalem:* Now as he was Man, he wept to see what temporal Judgments they would bring upon themselves.

But then, on the other hand, as he was God, he rejoiced at their eternal Destruction; for upon their despising those Declarations of his, he thereupon pronounces upon them eternal Wrath; calling such *Divels, Serpents, and a Generation of Vipers, and that*
they

Titus 2. 11.
Ephes. 1. 3.

John 10..27.

Mak 2..17.

Matt. 5. 45.

Luke 6. 6.
& 14. 14.

Matt 23. 33.
John 6. 7
Mat 3.7.& 13.
11. & 12. 34.

John 12. 40.

they should not escape the Damnation of Hell : And *John* the Baptift pronounced the like Sentence; and all the Apoftles had the like Power after they had received their Commiffion.

Matt. 5. 44.

As for that Saying of *Chrift*'s to them, *To Blefs,and Curs not* ; that was but when they were but private Believers; as alfo, it taught that Clemency, as *not to refift temporal Injuries* : But when they had received

Matt. 16. 19.

Luke 10. 16.

the Holy Ghoft, then was *the Keys of Heaven and Hell Committed to their Charge*; and they had Power by them, *to Bind and to Loofe, to Remit and to Retain*

Luke 20. 23.

Sin. What was that but Bleffing and Curfing? For

Pfal. 24. 7.

the Bleffing of a Commiffionated Prophet or Apoftle, it opens the Gate of Heaven; that is, it opens the Heart in Love, to that God that fent fuch a Meffage *of glad Tidings of Salvation* : So on the Contrary, the Curfe of a Prophet, it opens the Gate of Hell; That

Acts 7. 54.

is, it opens the Heart in Envy, Malice, and Revenge; and whofe Heart that fpiritual Key doth open no Man can fhut; and whofe Heart they fhut no Man can open.

Therefore it was that *Paul* faid, *That they were the*

1 Cor. 6. 2.

Heb. 10. 29.

Theff. 5. 20.

Saver of Life unto Life, unto thofe that believed them, and the Saver of Death unto Death unto thofe that defpifed them. Again, *Paul* and the reft of the Apoftles, did declare, *That whoever denyed the Faith of Jefus, or defpifed Prophefie, or turned Apoftate, that*

1 John 3. 8.

& 5. 16.

2 Cor. 2. 16.

there could be no Sacrifife for fuch Sins, neither were fuch to be Prayed for ; but upon the contrary, *to be fealed up unto eternal Death.*

All the Spiritual Declarations of the Prophets reach to the eternal State of Man, for they pointing at *their God's becoming Flefh*, and that, *upon his Death and Refurrection the eternal State of the Two Seeds of*

Faith

Faith *and* Reafon *takes being*; for the Refurrection of *Chrift* gains Power to raife the Dead, and give each Seed his Reward.

And therefore the Gofpel apropriates *David*'s Key to belong to it, which Key lyes in fuch and the like^{Pfal. 149. 4.} Sayings, *The Lord takes Pleafure in his People, he will beautifie the Meek with Salvation*; this is the Key that opens Heaven : And as follows, *Let the high Praifes of God be in their Mouth, and a two-edged Sword in their Hand*; and then with the other Key and Sword, *To execute Vengance upon the Heathen, and Punifhments upon the People*; *To bind their Kings with Chains, and their Nobles with Fetters of Iron*; *To execute upon them the Jndgment written* : And this is the Key that opens and none can fhut, and fhuts and no Man can open.^{Pfal. 149. 9.} *This Honour*, faith *David*, *belongs to all living Saints.* For thefe Keys and Sword belongs to all Saints; and^{Ifa 54. 17.} *David* himfelf, in thofe and the like Sayings, had^{& 57. 4.} flung into the Fire all that difpifed his Spirit of Prophefie, *of his God's becoming Flefh*, and Sealed them up in thefe Words; Saying, *divide their Tongues, for*^{Pfal. 55. 9.} *I have feen Violence in the City.* *Caft them down in thy Anger, Confume them in Wrath, let not them come into thy Righteoufnefs, blot them out of the Book of Life, and*^{Pfal. 59. 13.} *let them not be written with the Righteous*; *Let burning*^{Pfal. 140. 10.} *Coals fall upon them*; *let them be caft into the Fire.*

The Prophet *Jeremiah* likewife, meeting with the Seed of the Serpent, oppofing his fpiritual Declarations, concerning *God's becoming Flefh*, and his Sufferings by that Seed, Seals them up to Death Eternal; for they were for devifing Devifes againft that Doctrine of his; therefore he powereth forth thefe Imprecafions againft them; faing, *O Lord, forgive not*^{Jer. 18. 23. &} *their Iniquity, neither blot out their Sin from thy Sight,*^{19. 22.} &c.

&c. And then changing his Words, he fpeaks in

Jer. 23. 14.   the Perfon of God faying, *They are all unto me as* Sodom. So that we fee that the Prophit's Curfe is

Jer. 6. 30.   God's Curfe: And further faith he, *The Saints ſhall call them Reprobate Silver.*

This is Gofpel Power; the Lawes Curfe penetrates

Ez. k, 32. 24 down into the Grave, the firft Death ; but the Gof-
16. 27 29.   pels Power and Curfe raifes it again from the firft Death into a fecond and eternal Death ; being a living Death, and dying Life.

And thus we fee, that every true Minifter hath Power to fet Life and Death before Men: And that Mini-

Mark 16. 16.   ftry that hath not that Power, is no true Miniftry.
John 3. 18.   Now, what a blind Guide is this, that connot fee thefe plain Scriptures; but cries out, *Prove this by Scripture.* Woe be to all fuch as are led by thefe blind Guides! Oh, that all the Elect were but delivered from their Captivity and Bondage under their Formalities, and might come to hear of Truth ; that their Joy and Peace might abound, being the Seale of eternal Life.

But it is a wonderful thing, that fuch Preachers as thofe, who cannot Believe that any Prophet hath Power as aforefaid, and yet they themfeives fhall take upon them to Judge Mans Faith, and Condemn him for it. fo is it not a wicked thing to deny the Prophets and Apofiles Power of the Keys of Heaven and Hell, and yet prefume to do that thing themfelves, whilft they acknowledg themfeives but falible Men : Doth not this Make you juftly damned in your felves ? But it is no wondring at it, for what faith the Scripture,

John 12. 40.   *He hath blinded their Eyes, they Stumble at Noon-Day:* They have all the Spirit of Slumber.

And now I fhall return to Anfwer this Mifreprefentor's falfe Reflections upon our main Principles ; yea,
, fuch

such as the very Scriptures ſtands upon, and on which eternal Life wholy depends.

In Page the 18*th.* you bring in *John Reeve* ſciteing him thus; Saying, *God is not a Spirit, but hath a Body:* Your Reflections are thus.

The Accuſation.

The Scripture makes a Body and a Spirit Tow oppoſite things, ſo that a *Body is not a Spirit, nor a Spirit a Body* Eccles. 12. 7. *A Spirit hath not Fleſh and Bone,* Luke. 24. 37. The Scripture calls God *a Spirit,* but never *a Body*; God is not in form of a Man, but is inviſible, and no Man ever Saw him or can.

C H A P. VII.

ANSWER.

1. **Y**our Citation is falſe; For *John Reeve's* Words are thus, *That God is not a Spirit without a Body.* By your falſe Citation, you would have your worldly Diſciples to think, That he affirms, *That God is a Body without a Spirit.* But, to come to the Point; I muſt tell you, That the Body and Soul are not Two contrary Things; and if your *Solomon,* told you ſo with one Breath, he tells you the quite ^{Eccleſ. 3. 2.} contrary in another: But many times wiſe *Solomons,* Verſe 20. do not know the meaning of their own Sayings.

Solomon was a wiſe Man, but the Wiſdom which he 1 Kings 3. 12. craved, and that God gave him, was but natural; & 10 24 & 11. ſo that *Solomon's* Writings are but the Operations 4. of his natural Reaſon, and from ſome intrigate

E . Sayings

Sayings of his Father *David:* So they are no Scripture,
for he was no Prophetical Man.

Matt. 12. 42.

2. Again, If the Body and Soul are two contrary
things, (as you fay) and in Opofition to each other,
then was the Body and Soul of Chrift at variance,
with it felf; and in Opofition with each other, and
fo two opofite Things: If fo, then Chrift's Body did
not go to Heaven, nor never would: And belike,
you do not belive that Chrift's Body is in Heaven,
any more than the *Quakers*; and I know not how
you fhould believe it, becaufe your God hath never
a Body: So Chrift is none of your Fatherly God if
he have a Body.

Can a Spirit live and fubfift without a Body; where
do the Scriptures fay, That God is a Spirit without a
Body: Did not you learn your own Catechife, or if
you did, have you forgotten? doth it not teach (faying *)* to your Pupils, *That God is a Spirit, Or a jpiri-
tual Subftance, moft Holy, Wife, Juft and Infinite.*

Now if it be fo, that God hath a Subftance, then
he muft on neceffity have a Body: And if he be *Holy,
Wife, and Juft,* he muft have a Perfon to poffefs his
ravifhing Glory in, and yet to be of uncompounded

Ex d. 15. 2. Purity. Is it not faid, *That God was a Man of War*;
that fhews that he is in the form of a Man: Alfo
Chrift told the *Pharifes, That there was no Man per-*

Matt. 19. 17.
Joh. 5. 1. 3. *fectly Good but one, which was God.*

3. Moreover, if your Soul can be more Wife, Juft,
and Holy without your Body, then turn it out of the
Body, and fee what Holinefs and Juftice it can Act

1 Cor. 6. 19. without its Body.

But the Truth of Scripture is, That God had a

Revel. 21. 23.
& 1. 4 & 10. 1. Body and Perfon from all Eternity; a fpiritual Body, brighter than the Sun, more clear than Chrifti-
al.

al, and that is the Reafon why Mortality cannot be-^{Deut. 10, 6.} hold him as he is in his full Glory: If God was willing at any time that fome of his Servants, the Prophets, fhould behold him, he was compelled to vale his Glory, fo as that their frail Nature might be in a capafity to behold him.

And this we further affirm, That we can fooner find in Scripture, that our God hath, and ever had, a diftinct Body of himfelf, than you can find in Scripture a Trinity of Perfons in one Godhead; for if you find Three diftinct Perfons, then you muft find Three Bodies; and where then is your Spirit God become.

4. Again, is not the Scriptures clear, That the Fathers of old did fee God, and ever beheld him in^{Gen. 17. 2.} Form and Shape of a Man: Will you fay that God^{Exod. 24. 10.} ^{Ifa 6. 5.} affumed that Shape, and yet had no Shape of his own;^{John 36. 5.} this is to make God a Conniver.^{Exod. 33. 23.}

It is no wonder, as I faid before, that you difpife *John Reeve* for faying that the Lord fpake to him to the hearing of the Ear; for you do not believe that God hath any Tongue to fpeak at all: *For*, fay you, *a Spirit hath no Flefh, and hath no Body*: *For*, fay you, *Body and Spirit are Two contrary things.*

As the Scripture faith that God hath a Body, fo it^{Din. 7. 9.} attributes to this Body, Hands, Eyes, Face, Nofe,^{Revel. 10. 1.} Mouth, Ears, Arms, Leggs, Breaft, Heart, Back,^{& 1. 14.} ^{John 6. 5.} &c. And yet muft he have never a Body, this is^{Pfal. 94. 9} clearly to deny Scripture, for the Scripturian faith,^{Num. 12. 8.} *That God hath a Body*; but the Antefcripturian faith,^{Ifa. 65. 5.} *That God hath neither Body, Parts, or Shape, but yet is an infinite vaft God, filling all things, and is in all Places at one and the fame time, and fo can neither Affend nor Defcend, Come nor Go, but is everywhere at once*; as your great *Auguftin* faith.

E 2   This

This is yours and the Worlds monftrous God: Are thofe the Men that are fo capable of Argument; if we fhould be as ignorant in the Scriptures as you, it were no matter if our Tongues fhould cleave to the Roof of our Mouths.

I wonder you are not afhamed to pretend to Scripture; do you believe the Scripture? Certain I am, that there are many Doctors of your Church that doth not believe them at all; for inftance hereof, there is one of your Doctors, namely Dr. *More:* This Man, in one of his Books, called his *Cabila,* doth little lefs than give the Scripture the Ly; for treating upon the Creation of Man by *Mofes,* faith *That the Scriptures doth not always fpeak according to the exactnefs of Truth, but according to their Appearance in Senfe and the vulgar Opinion;* and he quotes *Chrifoftim, Bernard,* and *Aquinus,* as holding the fame things, and inftances it as to the Creating of *Adam* and *Eve:* Saying thus, *God hath no Figure or Shape,* altho Mofes *faith he hath;* he *only permits the Ignorant and Vulgar People to Believe fo, it being his Prudence and Policy fo to do.*

Now is not this Odious, for what Prudence is it to Flatter, Diffemble, and Deceive the People; for muft Gods Prophets be but like Polititians of State, pretending one thing, and acting another.

Again, this Man brings in *Mofes* fpeaking thus; *God took of the Duft of the Ground, wrought it with his Hands into fuch a temper that it was fit to make the Body of a Man; which when framed, then comes near to it with his Mouth, and breathed into his Noftrils the Breath of Life.*

And when God had made a Woman of one of Adam's *Ribs, he takes her by the Hand, and brought her to* Adam; *fo when* Adam *was awaked, he found his Dream to be*

true,

true, for he dream'd that God took a Woman out of him, for God flood by him with a Woman in his Hand.

Now it is true, fays this Doctor, *Moses* fpakes in this manner to fatisfy the rude Multitude, who was ever ready to think that God was in Forme and Shape as they were; and thus *Moses* complyed with their Humour, and permited them to belive fo; *yet,* faith he, *it is a Contradiction to the Idia of God, to have Figure and Shape.*

Now what fay you to this, is not this giving *Moses* the Lie? *Moses,* you fee, would permit People to believe, That God was in the Form of a Man: Now why will not you permit us to believe fo? *Moses* did not count this Doctrine a mifchievous Principle, as you do; but you, with this Man, fet your felves againft *Moses,* and againft the Scriptures; they are counted no other than a Lie with you: Now it is clear by this, that many of you Doctors are ftark blind Athifts.

your Proteftant Church is now grown as blind with Age, almoft as your Fathers the Papifts, and as Atheiftical as one of the Popes, who faid, *That that Fable of Jefus Chrift had brought their Church great Riches:* And one of that Church faid to me, *that the Scriptures were but balderdafh Stuff.*

Now as to that faying of Chrift's to his Difciples, *That a Spirit had not Flefh and Bone as he had;* it was only to inform them that there was no fuch Spirit as the World imagined, that could be feen, that had no Body; for Eyes of Flefh muft have a Subftance for its Object: Therefore faid Chrift, *handle me and fee, for I have a Body, a Subftance of very Flefh and Bone;* and they felt, and believed him to be their Lord and God. John 20. 27.

For

For Chrift, from hence, would have them for ever after to know that all Spirits, whither of God, Men, or Angels, are always invifible; for it is the Body that is vifible, for the Soul that is in it is always invifible, which Spirit comprehends all vifible things, yet cannot Live, Act, or Operate without its Body. And fo much for that Principle.

Again, Page 19*th.* you Reprefentor object againft that moft divine and mifterious Principle of God the Fathers becoming Flefh; and call this *a Doctrine quite contrary to Scripture,* and produce thofe Scriptures for Proof againft us; namely, *that God fent his Son made of a Woman, And the Word was made Flefh;* but, fay you, *there is not one Word, That the Father was made Flefh.*

C H A P. VIII.

ANSWER.

IT is confeffed by us, that the Scripture faith, *That God fent his Son,* as alfo, *that Chrift came of himfelf, and that he laid down his Life of himfelf.* Now if he laid down his Life of himfelf, then where was the Father but in himfelf; for it was his divine Spirit that was the Father, by which he could lay down his Life by that felf, and by that felf could take it up again: For God tranfmuteing his fpiritual Body into Flefh fo gained the Godhead and humane Nature together, and fo hath a' Twofold Self Humane and Divine.

Therefore, when he faith, *he hath Power of himfelf to lay down his Life,* then he fpeaks as in Referance to his

Gal. 4. 4.
John 5. 26.
& 10. 18.
Eph. 5. 2.

Heb. 1. 3.

Titus 2. 14.

his God-head; and when he faith, *That he can of him self do nothing,* and the like, then he fpeaks as in relation to his Manhood: God then hideing himfelf in that Manhood. *Ifa. 45. 15,21, 22,23. Compared.*

Again, if it be granted, That Chrift is God and Man, then it muft be acknowledged, That where Chrift is, there the Father is; and Chrift affirms it himfelf, faying, *That he that had him, had the Father, and he that had feen him, had feen the Father.* *John 14. 9. Gal. 1. 4. 1 Per. 2. 24.*

Now from all this, doth it not plainly appear, That he was the Father himfelf, as well as the Son: And *John* faith, *That in the Beginning was the Word, and the Word was with God:* And this Word was God; and that God, or Word became Flefh: Then furely that one God was Father as well as Son; unlefs you can prove there were Two Gods, or with the *Arians,* That Chrift was one with the Father in Union, but not in Effence; and if fo, then every Believer is as much God as Chrift is: But you have your Two Gods, one of which, you fay, took Flefh, the other did not; here you divide the Subftance. *John 1. 1. verfe 1.. Matt. 1. 20.*

What a Monfter do you here make of God; for you had before Chrifts Incarnation thofe Two Gods in Heaven, *a Father God, and a Son God;* and that Son you fay, *The Father Begot before all Worlds, and then was begot again in this World;* fo your God the Son was Twice Begot, or Twice Made: Is this good Sence, is this your Wifdom, is this good Divinity; nay, without all Controverfy, this is quite contrary to Scripture, and to fober Reafon alfo.

For was there ever any more than one God, and did not the Prophet *Ifaiah* fay; *That God would not give his Glory to another;* and yet it is faid, *That all the* *Zech. 14. 9. Deur. 6. 4. Ifaiah 42. 8. & 48 11. Pfal. 103. 20. Heb. 1. 6.*

Angels

Isaiah 45. 23.
Phil. 2. 10

Angels of God should Worship Christ, and that to him every Knee should bow; and that not only *in Earth,*but

Rev. 1. 22. 6.
Compar'd with
V. the 14.

in Heaven alfo : Who then could fhare with him, for he was the Lord God of all the Prophets, teftified by the Angel unto *John;* which Angel bid *John* worfhip God, even that God of the Prophets, which was no other but Jefus Chrift; Therefore it is faid, *I Jefus have fent my Angel, and behold I come quick'y,* &c.

1 J. 5. 2. 22.
& 5. 7.
2 J. 1. 7, 8.
Acts 4. 12.

There is no other God to come, no other Father, no other Refurrection and Life, no other Name or Power but Jefus Chrift our Lord, tho Men or Angels fhould gainfay it; as I have abundantly fhew'd in a Treatis intituled [*None but Chrift.*]

John 17. 3.

Moreover, to profecute this Principle a little further here, becaufe it is our Life and Foundation Principle, and it is impoffible for any Man to be faved that fhall prefumptuoufly difpife this Doctrin of Jefus being the everlafting Father after fo plain a Difcovery.

I am now to inquire how you *Trenitarians, Sofinians,* and *Arians,* bring Chrift in for your Saviour : You fay, *That by the Fall of* Adam *all Men had incurred Damnation, and fo were become God the Father's Debtors; and the Father ftanding upon Juftice would not be Reconciled with them, without the full payment of that Debt, as Life for Life. Now,* fay you, *the Father was fo far pleafed as to fend his Son, to pay the full Debt : And,* fay you, *this Son came voluntarily and paid the Debt; and by this means fatisfied the Wrath of his Father, and fo purchafed your Life by his Ranfom.*

Wherefore, if it be fo as you Teach, That the Father is diftinct from that Son, then are you not beholding to the Father at all : For take this Similitude for the Eluftration thereof; Suppofe, *I owe a Man*

a 1000

a 1000 *Pounds, or more, and I have not wherewith to pay him, and he will not forgive me any of the Debt; or I muft either pay it all, or to Prifon; there to remain till I have paid the utmoft Farthing; The Son of this my Creditor fees the Strait I am in, Commiferates my Cafe; fteps in voluntarily, and pays the Father the full Debt, and fo fets me at Liberty.*

'Now in this Cafe, who am I moft beholding to, the Father, or the Son; not to the Father at all, for he was for Juftice, and I wanted Mercy: The Son therefore was my Friend, and to him only am I bound, and him only am I to Love, Serve, and Obay.

This is the very plain Cafe; it is the Son Chrift Jefus that all the Elect Seed of *Adam* are beholding to, and not to any Father that either is, or ever was diftinct from him: But the Father of Chrift was his own Godhead Spirit, which through his eternal Love to the Seed of his own Body, was moved to change his Spiritual Body, (which was his everlafting Son) into Flefh, to the end he might be capable to dye, and fhed his Blood for their Redemption; as alfo, that he might have Power to raife the Seed of the Serpent to a Second and eternal Death, for their Cruelty acted againft him and his Elect Seed.

Phil. 3. 8.
Ephe. 6. 24.
1 Cor. 16. 22.
1 Tim. 6. 15.
Revel. 5. 12.
John 17. 5.
2 Cor 5. 19.
2 John 9.
John 8. 36.
1 Pet 1. 19.
& 2 Pet. 6.
Heb 2. 14.

Therefore his coming in Flefh was foretold by *Ifaiah,* and all the other Prophets; and that the Son that was to be born of a Virgin, *fhould in time be called the mighty God, and everlafting Father:* Now at this time this Prophefy is fulfilled, and by this Commiffion of the Spirit, he is both called and known to be the high and mighty God, and everlafting Father: This Scripture is poffitive, and fhall command all primative Scriptures to bow down to it.

Ifaiah 9. 6.

F   Thus

Thus the Scriptures are clear, to all that are a ppinted to Salvation, that Chrſt Jeſus is that one only, and alone true God, and everlaſting Father : To this the Holy Patriacks agree, obſerve their Teſtimony, which is conſonant to Scripture, being grounded upon Enoch's Propheſy.

Sim ſhall be gloriſied, when the great Lord God of *Iſſrael* appeareth on the Earth as a Man to ſave *Adam*; for God taking a Body upon him (namely of Fleſh and Bone) and eating with Men, ſhall ſave Men.

Ye ſhall ſee God in the ſhape of a Man (ſaid *Zebulon*) *he is the Saviour, he is the* [Father] *of Nations* ; *he that Believeth in him ſhall certainly Reign in Heaven*, ſaith *Levy and Judeth.*

God ſhall appear and dwell amongſt Men upon Earth, to ſave *Iſrael*; the Higheſt ſhall viſit the Earth, eating and drinking as Man with Man ; he ſhall ſave *Iſrael*: That is, God hiden in Man.

At the laſt Day we ſhall riſe, every one of us, to his own Scepter, ſaith *Benjamin*, *Worſhiping the King of Heaven, which appeared in the baſe Shape of a Man* ; *and as many as believed in him ſhall Reign with him at that time* : And all faithful Men ſhall riſe again, and the Reſidue to Shame, becauſe they believed not in God that came in the Fleſh to deliver.

Thus it is made Clear, That God the Father became Fleſh; but one Evidence more from *John*, befor I conclude this Point : He, in Admiration of his Lords Love cryed out ſaying, *O What Love the Father hath beſtowed upon us, but the World knoweth him not, but we know him.*

1 John 3. 1.

Now, who was this Father of Love, was it any other but the Apoſtles Jeſus; his following Words doth ſhew it as clear as the Light ; ſaying thus, We

Wᴇᴇ

who are his Apoftles do know him ; and we further
know, that when [*He*] doth appear we fhall be like
him ; for we fhall fee him as he is : That is, when Pfal 3. 21,
he comes to change our vile Bodies, and make them
like his own glorious Body, then fhall we fee him as
he is in himfelf, one perfonal God Cloathed with Flefh
and Bone, as a Garment of eternal Glory.

This is the Faith (faith *John) That maketh Pure,*
and he whofe Faith abides in Jefus Chrift, that came
by Water and Blood, hath the everlafting Father;
and he that holdeth this Faith fineth not : That is,
he fineth not to Act; he may have the motion to Sin,
but it preferveth from the Act; for that golden Grace
of Faith crufheth that *Cokatrice Egg* of the Motion of
Sin, before it become a ftinging Serpent, and fo Con-
quers and Overcomes.

This is the Doctrin of the Gofpel, and he that
Imbraceth it hath the Father and the Son, where and 2 John 10 9.
to whom the Bleffing and the Salvation of God-fpeed
is given : This is the true God, and the Amen, and 1 John 5. 20.
all other Gods are Idols. Revel 3. 14.

This is the *Muggletonian's* Principle, which the
Ante-Scripturian calls a mifchievious Principle. Thus
you curfe the true God, and defy the Holy one of
Ifrael, chufing to your felf a God of your own lying
Imagination.

In Page 19. you further Object againft that Principle, *how that the God-head dyed.* This, fay you, is
quite contrary to Scripture, which faith, *God is
Immortal, and that he hath Immortality* 1. Tim. 1. 17.
& 6. 16. Alfo, you fay, That *Muggleton* teacheth,
That the Soul of Man is Mortal, and turns to Duft : To
this, fay you, the Scripture tells us, *That the Souls of
Men are alive after their Death.* Matt. 22 : 32. And,

F 2 *that*

that God is said to be their God after they are Dead, Matt. 10. 28. *And that we are not to fear them that can kill the Body and not the Soul.* And that *Lazarus,* when he dyed, went to Heaven, and *Dives* to Hell, *Luke* 16. 22.

C H A P. IX.

A N S W E R.

Acts 10. 28.   The Scriptures, say *that God purchased the Church with his Blood* : Now the Blood of Chrift was no other but the Blood of God, and when he power'd forth that Blood, then did he power forth his Life ; for Life lay in that Blood.

Ifaiah 53. 12.   Therefore it is said *That he powered forth his Soul un-*
Heb 9. 14.   *to Death, and that he offered up himself through the eter-nal Spirit :* What is that, but that the eternal Spirit entered into Death, or paffed through Death, in a Moment, into eternal Life ; Death being too weak
Coll. 2. 9.   to keep him under ; fo that whatever Life was in Je-
1 Cor. 15. 54.   fus did enter into Death.

Revel. 1. 18.   Therefore he that was the *Alpha* and *Omega,* the *Firft* and the *Laft,* was Dead, but is now Alive ; and behold he now lives for ever more, and is that immortal only wife God, blessed for ever : So that we do
1 Tim. 6. 16.   affirm , That God is immortal ; and we also know
2 John. 7.   that Eternity did become Time, for Flefh was in Time,
Revel. 1. 18.   and Time did become Eternity again.

Now, in that you Teach, That God cannot dye ; it is evident that you do not belive that Chrift was a-ny ny God at all ; fo that you *Trenitarians, Arians,* and *Socinians,* you are all a like, and that you are no more Chriftians then they : For it will neceffarily follow, That if it were nothing but humane Nature, or Life in Chrift, that died, then the Death of any other Man had been equevolent to Chrift's Sufferings, and as Meritorious as his ; and fo your Spirit God, without a Body, might have faved you by fheding of any other Man's Blood.

But the true *Chriftian* doth know that no Blood can make *Attonement* for *Sin,* but the moft precious and unvaluable *Blood of a God* ; to believe this, is to drink his *Blood* : And to believe that that *bleffed Body of his* was no lefs then the very body of God, this is to eate his *flefh* ; fo that whofoever eats his *flefh,* and drinks his *blood* fo, hath by fo doing gained the full affurance of *Eternal Life* ; this is a ftanding Truth, and fhall prevail. John 6. 54.

But how is it poffible you fhould believe this, when as you cannnot believe that any Life dies at all ; for fay you, *The Soul of Man is alive after Death* ; here your Ignorance appears very great for all your Learning ; Where did you ever find by Scripture, *That the Soul of any man was ever alive without its body ?* The Scripture no where affirms it, if rightly underftood ; they are but old Wives Fables, or Monks and Fryers Forgeries, and heathenifh Principles from their own blind Imaginations.

As for thofe Sayings concerning *Dives* and *Lazarus,* 'tis but a Parable, and fo muft have a Spiritual meaning; for Souls without Bodies have no Tongues, nor Eyes, nor Bofoms, as that Parable fpeaks of ; but that Parable was only to fet forth the two Seeds here in Mortality, which is largely opened by this Commiffion of the Spirit.   And Luke 16.

And as to Chriſt ſpeaking of *God being the God of the living, and not of the dead,* it was ſpoken to the *Saduces,* who denyed the Reſurrection ; therefore Chriſt ſhews that there was a neceſſity of a Reſur-

Act 2. 31. rection, ſeeing that *Abraham, Iſaac,* and *Jacob,* and the and 13. 36. reſt of the Prophets were dead, and their Sepulchres are with us at this day ; and if God do not raiſe them again to that Glory their Faith was pitch'd upon, then was he the God of the dead, and not of the living, in that all dyed to him inſtead of living to him.

And as to that ſaying, *Fear not them which can kill the body, &c.* That is, fear not him that may kill both Soul and Body by a natural death, but rather fear him that hath an abſolute power in himſelf to ſlay both Soul and Body with an Eternal or ſecond Death.

Moreover, when the Scripture ſaith the body dies, doth not that include the ſoul, or natural Life? What have you your natural Learning for, but to underſtand the natural ſence of words? Do you not find, that that which our Tranſlation calls body, the Greek calleth ſouls ? as *Numb.* 6. 6. there it is ſaid, *That he ſhall come at no dead body,* in our Bible ; but after the Greek, your own Doctors read thus ; *He ſhall come at no dead Soul.*

Gen. 2. 17.   Is it not ſaid, *That man was made a living ſoul ?* And was not the threatning charge given out, *That that* Ezek. 18. 4 *ſoul that ſinned, that ſoul ſhould dye ?* and yet ſay you, verſ. 20. the ſoul cannot dye.

Now that which the National Miniſtry do make a ground of the Immortality of the ſoul, is to all ſpiritual wiſe men, an evident proof of its Mortality ; as where it is ſaid, *ſo ſuch a one dyed, and was gathered to his people* ; now whether is it, that they were gathered but into the grave ? As for inſtance, ſee 2 *Kings* 22. 20.   If

If the Soul can enjoy Heaven without its body, what matter of a Refurrection? but it is certain that the Scriptures affirms the contrary, and that there can be no Salvation without a Refurrection. *Col. 3. 4. 1 Thef. 4.14.*

When *God* shall raife the dead, he hath his Angels attending to gather the Saints together, as *God* raifeth them; neither *God* nor his Angels doth not bring their Souls from Heaven to affume their dead bodies; but our *God* raifeth Soul and Body together, out of the *Grave* by a word fpeaking, as he did the *Body* and *Soul* of *Lazarus*. *Mat. 13. 41. c. 24. 31. c. 25. 31. John 5. 28. c. 11. 43.*

Again, on the other hand, muft all the damned Souls come from Hell to fetch up their curfed bodies? What Hell do they come from, but out of the Grave, Soul and Body out of the Grave; and when the Soul and Body rifes, then the Devil rifes to his eternal Punifhment; and this Earth will be the place of the Devils Torment, where he acted all his Lies and Cruelty; there fhall he fuffer eternally (after the Elect Men and Angels are affended with their God into Eternal Glory) the Plagues of *Egypt* were a Tipe of this. *Revel. 20. 13. Ifa. 66. 24. Jer. 17. 13. Mich. 7. 11. Exod. 10. 21. Revel. 10. 10.*

Thefe things will be fo in their time: And fo much in anfwer to this Principle.

In *pag.* 20*th.* you oppofe *John Reeve* for faying, How that *but one Angel fell from his Created Purity and Glory.*

This Doctrine, fay you, is quite contrary to *Scripture*; which tells us in *Jude*, That *the Angels fell*: and this, fay you, cannot be apply'd to *Kain* and his Pofterity: For they, fay you, *by our own words never fell*: And as for *Kain*, fay you, *He never was from that fallen Angel, but was of* Adam's *begetting as well as* Seath. And again you affirm alfo, *That all* Kain's *Offspring perifhed in the Floud.* *The Accufation*

C H A P.

CHAP. X.

ANSWER.

Ifa. 29. 10.
John 12. 40.
Rev. 11. 7.

IF that Offspring of that Serpent-Angel that was caft from Heaven could know it felf, then you might know that thefe *Angels* fpoken of in *Jude* were the Offspring of Curfed *Kain*, the Serpent Angel tranfmuted into Flefh, and referved in Chains of Unbelief, and the Darknefs of Ignorance: For *Jude* fpoke of no other Devils but what were clothed in Flefh; and it was they that were the Devils ordained to condemnation. '

And therefore mind; for he brings in *Sodom* and *Gomorrah*, and the Rebellious *Jews* againft *Mofes*, and thofe upftart Hypocrites who denied the Lord to be the only and alone true God, and yet pretended his Name : All thefe, faith he, were ordained to condemnation in that *Serpent-Angel* aforefaid, being re-probated in the Seed; and *Kain* was that Seed. And therefore *Jude* pronounces the Woe unto them, as the Off-fpring and Seed of *Kain*, to whom Eternal Torment doth belong.

v. 11.

Rev. 12. 7.

Again, where it is faid, that *there was a war in hea-ven, Michael and his Angels fighting againft the Dragon and his Angels* : That *Michael* was the Spirit of the Lord Jefus in all his Angelical Believers; and the Dragon was the Spirit of Curfed *Kain*, in all his Seed. This War was on Earth, tho' faid to be in Heaven, becaufe the Original of both Seeds came from Heaven; for there never was any actual Rebelli-on in Heaven, but that Angel-Serpent aforefaid being
··   caft

caft out, all his Seed fell in him; and was caft out
with him, and fo actual Rebellion took place: And
therefore, faid *John, Wo to the Inhabitants of the Earth,*
for the Devil not Devils *is come down amongft you.* Verfe 12, 17.
And it was this Devil that brought the Wo, both to
Saint and Serpent; in this Warfare doth thefe Two
Woes take place to them Two Seeds; one in this
Fight having his Heel bruifed, which is in Perfecuti- Gen. 3. 15.
on, lofs of Goods, and Death natural; the other Rev. 13.7.10.
having his Head bruifed by the Saints Weapons of
War, which reacheth to a fecond Death.

And this Devil that was caft down, was the Fa- 1 John 3. 12;
ther of *Cain,* from whence all *Wickednefs* and *Cruel-*
ty hath flown; for *Cain* was the very *Firft-born* of that
Devil, and the fulnefs of that *Serpent-Angel's-God-Head*
lived Boddily in *Cain*, and fuch of his Seed, that
have in them a great Share of that piercing Reafon,
of *God-head-power,* became potent Angels, Lords and
Governours of this World, it being given to that
Seed; and they labour in this their Kingdom, to imi-
tate the grandure of that Glory their Father, the
fallen Angel, had before his Fall, and to come as near
to it as poffibly they can.

And here it is, That the Prophet *Ezekiel* compares Ezek. 29. 3.
Pharaoh King of *Egipt* to the great red *Dragon*: And
the *Affirian* Monarch was faid by the Prophet, *to be*
in Dignity, Power, Glory and Buty, like unto his Fa- Chap. 31. 3.
ther the Angel before his Tranfmutation into Flefh, when
he walked once in the Garden of Eden, *being greater than*
feveral others of his Father's Children: The great Kings
of *Babilon* were faid to be, *from* Lucipher, *and therefore*
were called after his Name, Lucipher *the Sun of the Mor-* Ifa. 14. 2.
ning : And they are faid by the Prophet *Ifaiah, To be*
caft down from Heaven, which could not be, if they
G   had

had not proceeded from the *fallen Angel..*

And as they were cast down from Heaven in that *Angel,* even so they were for exalting their Thrones above the Stars, and to be like unto God; which doth shew, That they were evil Kings, and evil Beasts For good Kings, and such as proceed not from *Cain,* they are not for exalting themselves so high, as to that Heavenly Throne of judging of Mens *Faith* and *Conscience*; neither will they tiranise over their Subjects, but do Justice according to the Law. But to the Matter aforesaid.

Ezek: 28. 3.   The great King of *Tyrus,* seems to out-top all the foregoing Kings with *Angelical* Perfection; for he is said to be the *very anointed Cherub himself*; he having as great a Share of that lost Glory as his fallen Nature could afford him; for that *Angel* that he proceeded from was a *Cherub,* which was the highest Order of *Angels*; and this King was of the highest Degree of Wisdom, Buty, and Glory: And therefore *Verse 13. 14.* his Perfections was such, as that he was said to be *Wiser than* Daniel; by which Wisdom he had goten him Riches of Gold and Silver in abundance; as also in his *Kingdom* all sorts of cunning Arts and Siances, and a great Merchant, mighty in Traffick: All this from his Father the *Angel.*

Therefore, said the Prophet to this Prince, *Thou hast been in* Eden, *the Garden of God*; *every presious Stone was thy Covering*; *yea, the Tabret and the Pipe was prepared in thee in the Day that thou wast Created:* This was not *Adam,* but the *Angel,* &c.

Again, *Thou art the anointed* Cherub *that covereth, and I have set thee so.* (Again, faith the Prophet) *Thou wast upon the Holy Mountain of God, and hast walked in the midst of Stones of Fire : Thou wast perfect*

in

in thy Ways from the Day thou wast Created, till Iniqui- Verse 15.
*ty was found in thee: Thou hast corrupted thy Wisdom, by
reason of thy Brightness.*

Now can this Prince of Reason, (so exalted) be de-
rived from any other Roote, but that *Angelical Reprobate, That was cast down from Heaven for his Pride,
in those his great Perfections:* Therefore his Wisdom is Matt.
said, *to excel* Daniel*'s:* And so it might be said to
excel *Adam's* too.

Therefore these Princes are not related to *Adam,*
but to that *Angel,* that corrupted his Wisdom of pier-
sing Reason; for had his Wisdom flow'd from Faith's
Nature, it could not have Corrupted it self; but the
Wisdom of Reason is subject to Sin : Yea, Reason it
self, (tho so noble a Nature, and splendant, if not
upheld by that Power that Created it) is Sin it self;
and here is the *Off-spring* and *Root* of all fleshly Glory:
So that, that which is adored for a God is damned
for a Devil. *If this gives Offence, I cannot help it :
But to proceed.*

Again, Whereas you, (the Opposer of the *Muggletonians* Principles) say, First, *That* Cain *was of*
Adam*'s begeting;* And then Secondly, *That all* Cain*'s
Off-spring perished in the Flood :* These are both abso-
lutely false : For,

First, It is evident, That *Adam* never begot *Cain,*
neither do the Scriptures affirm it, if rightly under-
stood : For tho *Moses* saith, *That* Adam *knew* Eve *his* Gen. 4. 1,
Wife, and she conceived and bare Cain ; yet *Moses* doth
not say, *That she conceived* Cain *of* Adams *Seed :* And
therefore in the very next Words after, *Moses* hath
these Words [*And she again bare his Brother* Abel.] Verse 2.
Without mentioning a Word of his knowing of her
after; and this was to keep the Seeds of aspiring Rea-

son

The Muggletonian *Principles Prevailing,*
fon in the dark; for *Eve* had conceived *Cain* of the
Serpent Angel, before ever *Adam* knew her; and that
was it that made her full of Luft after her Innocent
Husband.

Again, To clear this further, Doth not the Apoftle *John* fay, *That* Cain *was from that* Serpent-Angel,
which he calls by the name of Wicked one. Now dare
you fay , *That* Adam *was that* Wicked one, *from
whence (* as *John* faith) *the Spirit of* Cain *fprung:* Sure-
ly no; for that were Wickednefs indeed to Men that
profefs Scripture.

Furthermore, *Cain* and *Abel,* altho they are faid to
be Brothers, yet their Brotherhood comes but by the
Mother's fide, even as it is apparent, that *Hely* and
Jacob, the Two attributed Fathers of *Joseph,* the Huf-
band of *Mary,* were Brothers by the Mother's fide.
Now it is worth the minding here, That *Joseph*
could not be the natural Son of both thofe Men;
for obferve in the *Genealogy* of our Saviour, *Matthew*
makes *Mathan* to be the Father of *Jacob,* and *Jacob*
the Father of *Joseph* : But *Luke* makes *Melchi* the Father of *Hely,* and *Hely* the Father of *Joseph.*
Now here is a different Race; for *Jacob,* the natural Father of *Joseph,* he proceeded from *Solomon,* but
Hely fprung from *Nathan,* and was *Joseph's* Father by
Law or Title, but not by Nature.

Therefore, as *Hely* was the fuppofed Father to *Jo-
feph,* and *Joseph* the fuppofed *Father* of *Chrift;* even
fo was *Adam* no more than the fuppofed *Father* of *Cain*;
nay he is no where called the *Father* of *Cain,* not in
all the Scriptures: But on the contrary, that *Cain's*
Father was called that *Wicked one,* or *Devil;* for
Wicked one and *Devil* are both of one fignification.
See and Compare, *Matt.*13.19. *Luke* 8.12. *Mark* 4.15.

Therefore

1 John 3. 12.

Matt. 1. 15.

Luke 2. 23.

Therefore it is without all Controverſy, That *Adam* was not that *Wicked One, Satan,* or *Devil,* that begot *Cain*: Nay your own Doctor *Ainſer,* upon *Geneſis* ſaith, *That* Cain *was from the Devil;* and he citeth ſome of the *Hebrew* Doctors for Proof of the ſame: Saying; *That they Teach how that* Cain *was born of the Filth, and Seed of the Serpent, which was conveyed into* Eve: And that one *Menacham,* a Jewiſh Rabi ſaith, *That unto this World there cleaveth the ſecret Filthineſs of the Serpent, which came upon* Eve; *and becauſe of that Filthineſs Death is come upon* Adam, &c. But no more of this here, having wrote largely upon it in a Treatis Intituled, *Truth's Triumph,* or the *Witneſs to the Two Witneſſes,* which may ſome time come to publick view.

Secondly, as it is proved that *Adam* did not beget *Cain*; ſo it is falſe for you to ſay; *That all* Cain's *Off-ſpring periſhed in the Floud.* Now you that affirm this, will find it to the contrary; for if that had been ſo as you ſay, then there would be no Damnation for any that have been borne ſince.

But tho *Cain* was dead, and moſt of his *Off-ſpring,* yet his Seed was alive in curſed *Ham*; ſo that the Curſe given to the Serpent-Angel in the Womb of Eve run in a Line, even from *Cain* to *Ham,* and ſo to *Iſhmael* and *Eſau,* and ſo on to the end of the World: For altho *Ham* was begot by *Noah,* a good Man, and an elect Veſſel, yet was not *Ham* of that good Seed; for *Noah* had in him Two Seeds, as all Men elſe have, ſince *the Sons of God ſaw the Daughters of Men, and took them Wives of ſuch as were the Seed of* Cain: And ſo the Seed of *Adam* and that Seed of *Cain,* through Copulation, did perticipate of each others Seed; and which Seed is uppermoſt in Conception, that Seed grows

Gen. 9. 25. & 3. 14. Compared.
Iſa. 1. 4. & 14. 20.
Deut. 5. 5.
Gen. 6. 2.
Mat. 13. 25.

Matt. 10. 37. grows to be Lord over the other; and so a Man comes to have his Denomination according to the Predominancy of his Seed : And thus it was with *Ham*, for *Cain*'s Seed was predominant in *Ham*'s Conception.

John 8. 38.
33. 37. 44. So it was with those *Jews* that boasted themselves to be of *Abraham* : And tho they might be *Abraham*'s Seed according to the Flesh, yet Christ branded them for *Devils*, telling them, *That the Devil was their Father* : Which was no other than *Cain*, being the first Lyer and Murtherer.

Now, from hence, all sober Men may see, that a *Devil* and a *Saint* is all one to you; for you can find but one Scripture Seed; for God and Devil, Heaven and Hell, Saint and Serpent, with you come all from one Root.

Now, seeing it is so with you, I would advise you to leave off playing the Hipocrite, and forbear telling your Hearers, *That any of them will be Damned*: For if there be but one Seed, and that Seed the Seed of *Adam*, then all will be saved; so deal plainly to your People, and Preach to them general Redemption, and prove it from *Paul*'s Words, where he saith,

1 Cor. 15. 22. *That as in* Adam *all dye, so in Christ shall all be made alive.*

But will yea, or nill yea, this we must tell you,
Rom. 9. 27. *That there is a Seed, namely* Cain *and his* Off-spring,
Mat. 9. 13. *that never fell in* Adam, *but in the* Serpent-Angel, *and*
2. Pet. 1. 12. *so are uncapable of ever being Redeemed by Christ* : For
John 17. 9.
1 Tim. 2. 4. when on Earth, he never prayed for them : For tho
Matt. 18. 11. he wonld have all Men saved, yet it is but all those
& 10. 6.
Rom. 11. 26. that fell in *Adam*, that he hath any spiritual Salvation for.

This

This is that which makes that Seed fret themfelves, and call it a mifchevious Principle; and it will prove Mal. 3. 15. fad to that mifchevious Man that Condemns true Prophefy; and the true Believers thereof; as like-wife, that juftifieth the Seed of the Wicked to be the Ifa. 5. 20. Seed of *Adam*, who was the Seed of God.

Your farther Accufation Runs thus.

In *Pag.* 20. You fay, *That there is a Devil diftinct from Man, and would feem to prove it from that* Devil *that tempted* Chrift; *which you would have to be a bo-dily-Spirit; and you fcoff at wicked Imagination being the* Devil: And from hence you query from that Scrip-ture, ˙ *Mark* 5. 4. Saying, *Doth Imagination break Chains,* &c. And that their affirming, *That* Ely *fhould be* Chrift's *Reprefentative:* This you call all Fable.

CHAP. XI.

A N S W E R.

IF you will have a *Devil* without a Body, you muft go feek out a new-found World, to find out your unknown *Devil*: The Works of this *Devil* are ma-nifeft, and yet you cannot know him; for is there any Wickednefs in this World but what flows from that Carnal Spirit of Men and Women; who is a Revel. 8. 2. Kingdom of Wickednefs in that *Tophet* or Bodies of Mat.15; 19. Gal. 5. 19. theirs; for it is the Heart where the Court is kept, and is the only Nuffery of all evil Spirits conciv'd there by Imagination.   Oh!

Oh! the depth of this Imagination in this its bottomless Pit, and the uncleanness of the same : Do but compare Scripture, and in it we may find a very Pit-Devil : *All the Imaginations of Mans Heart,* (faith God) *are Evil, and continually Evil* : What's that but the Devil. And hath not this continual Work its first Formation in the Heart, being its own Work from its own Seed ; and its Worke is in this manner following.

Gen. 6. 5.
Jam. 4. 5, 6.
Isaiah 32. 6.
Jer. 17. 9.

For this is to be minded, That as the Spirit of Faith in the Heart of Man, is the Womb or Mother, for the Revelation of Faith to beget a Son out of the Seed of Faith.

So likewise the Seed of Reafon is the Womb or Mother, for Imagination to beget a Son or familier Spirit, for all evil Spirits are conceived in the Heart : If Envy be conceived, then Murder is brought forth ; if Luft be conceived, then Adultery is brought forth ; and if a familiar Spirit is conceived, then it brings forth fuch a Spirit as fpeaks forth *Motional Voices* and if by its Transformation into Angelical Light, then as falfe Prophets, it produces Vifions, Revelations, and internal Voices within them : Now this familiar Spirit is nothing elfe but a Witch ; fo that when it *Motions* forth Spiritual or Religious Matters, then it becomes fpiritual Witchcraft, and when it *Motions* forth upon a Temporal Account, then it becomes natural Witchcraft : The one or other of thefe Witchcrafts almoft all the World lies under.

James 1 15.
& 2. 15 16.
James 4. 1.

Jer. 23. 16.
Ifaiah. 8. 19.
Deut. 18. 10

Eph. 6. 12.

Therefore it follows, That this familiar Spirit that is begot by Imagination, doth fometimes produce fuch a Voice in it felf, as if fome Spirit without them did appear to them without Bodies, and Reveal things to them, as it was by the Witch of *Endor,* and as *Samuel* fpoke in *Saul's* Confience.   This

1 Sam. 28. 1.

This hath been a common thing in all Ages, and Gilt of Confcience can quickly quine an Object, and produce a motional Voce, thinking it is without the Body, whenas all is but from the *Familiar Spirit*.

And when this *Familiar Spirit*, or *new begot Wifdom* is quickened in the *evil Heart*, it grows from Strength to Strength, from one degree of Knowledg, to a further degree of evil Knowledg and evil Wifdom, *Creating* to it felf fuch *things* as God never *Created*; as *an immortal Soul, or Spirit, without a Body* : And it hath made it fo, as that it can appear in any Shape, Form, or Likenefs, whether it be *God*, *Man*, *Devil*, or *Angel*: All are made *Spirits* without *Bodies*.

Alfo it hath *Created* to it felf, fuch a *Devil* as can *whip* into Man, and out of Man, at his Pleafure: And when *Sin is Commited*, then all the *Evil* is charged upon that *boddilis Devil* : And yet Men muft be hanged for *Murder*, whenas, they fay, it is a *bodilis Devil* that is the *Murtherer*, or temps to *Murther*.

And more then this, *the Devil muft be chained in Hell-fire*; and yet a *bodilis Spirit*, and in all places at one time, where he can tempt all the *World* to *Sin*, and yet no body can fee *him*; *and yet he is in Hell-fire in Chains, but may be called out at the Pleafure of a Witch*: This is the *Worlds Bugbare Devil, and the pitchy Darknefs all the World lies under.*

Thus we fee what *Fruits* the *Imagination* of *Reafon* brings forth : And whereas you fcoffingly ask, *whether* Imagination breaks *Chains*, pointing to that faying of the Gofpel.

Here you fhew your *Ignorance*, that cannot *diftinguifh* between *Devils in Nature*, and *Devils produced by Accidents in Nature* : Nay, you know nothing at
H all,

Exod. 1. 10.
Jer. 4. 22.

Mark 5. 4.

all, of *neither* the one nor the other, and fo make no *difference of their Actions.*

For tho *Diftempers* in nature are *devilifh,* yet not *damned Devils :* For this we find, that *Chrift* never called *diftracted* or *mad Men Devils ;* for thefe may come through fome *extraordinary Fright, Grief,* or *Lofs ;* and in fome may *increafe* to that *ftrength,* as to break *Iron Chains:* For having broke the *Brain,* the Seat of *Reafon* is quite out of order, and fo makes them more ftrong then when their Reafon was in Order. And *Chrift* never Judged and Condemned thefe, but caft thofe *fiery Diftempers,* and *divilifh Difeafes* out, and reftored them to their *right Mind.*

So that it is not the *Diftracted* or *Unreafonable* that *Chrift* Condemned, but the *Learned,* and *Senfible,* and *Prudent Man ;* even fuch as *commit Murder for Confcience fake, and condemn true Prophefy,* from their *conceated Wifdom of high-flown piercing Reafon:* This is *evident* throughout all the *Scriptures,* efpecially in the Learned *Scribes* and *Pharifees, Who held a Counfel, and Reafoned in themfelves how they might intrap* Jefus *in his Words.*

Mark 1. 6.
Luke 20.2 0.
Matt. 26. 3.
Luke 20, 5.

And that *Devil* that tempted *Chrift,* he was one of them, and no fuch *bodilu Devil* as your Reafon hath created to it felf, that fhould carry *Chrift* up to the *Pinacle* of that *outward material Temple* in *Jerufalem,* no, no: But againft all your *Wifdom* of *Reafon,* we affirm, *That he was a Man-Devil, being a Learned* Scribe, *well Read in* Scripture, *and could argue the fame from this Pinacle of his fubtil Pate ;* but *Chrift* repulfed his *Scripture Argument* with *Scripture* again, faying, *It is written, thou fhalt not temp the Lord thy God, but him only thou fhalt ferve.*

Now

Now where was this *Scripture written,* was it not in *Deut.* 6. 13, 16? And was it not *writen* to Men *indued* with the *Wisdom* of *Reason?* It was not *writen* to a *bodilis Devil*; for *bodilis Devils* do not commit *Murder, Adultery,* or *tempt God,* it is *Man* that doth all this; and it was to *Man* that the Law was given, and so the Law saith, *Thou shalt not Tempt the Lord thy God, as your Fathers tempted him* : And again, *You shall not corrupt yourselves.* Exod. 20. & Deut. 4.:3. 1. Pfal. 78. 18 & 41.56.

Now, from what is here said, it must needs follow, that if *Pride, Envy, Lust, Covetuousness,* and *Hipocrisy* be the *Divels* in *Men,* are not *Men* and *Women* those *Devils* that are brought under the Power of those *Evils* : When the Apostle said, *That . the Devil should cast some of them Saints into Prison*; the Saints were not cast into Prison by *Devils* that had no Bodies. James 1. 14. & 4. 1. 2. 7. Compared. Revel. 2. 10.

Therefore lay not your Brats at other Mens Dores, but charge your own Souls home with the *Evil* you do; *For as it is* Man's *own* Soul *that Sins, so it is his own* Soul *that must suffer.* John 6. 70. & 8. 44. Acts 13. 10, Ifaiah 3. 9.

This will prove true, and so will that of *Moses* and *Elias,* altho you call it all *Fable* : For why will you ty God up to your *Imagination of cursed Reason?* Is anything too hard for God to do, when his *divine Wisdom* moves him to it? Did not he Swear by himself, to himself, what he proposed to do? And may he not, by the same Rule, change his own glorious Condition into Flesh; and having humbled himself to himself, may he not cause his *Humanity* to Pray and Cry unto his *Divinity* within him, or to his spiritual Charge, committed unto his Angels, without him, for a further Manifestation of his unserchable Power in Shame and Weakness, as well as in Power and Glory. Gen. 22. 16. Pfal 8. 5. Phill. 2. 7, 8. John 17. 5 19. Matt. 27. 46. & 28. 2. Luke 24. 4. Acts 1. 10. Revel. 22. 9.

Is

Is it not writen, How *that his Angels had given them a Charge to watch over him?* And did not *Moses* and *Elias* do so, from his Birth to his Affention? Alfo is

Luke 1. 17.
Matt. 4. 5.
Mall. 4. 5.
Matt. 17. 12. 3.

it not written, *That* John *the Baptiſt came in the Spirit and Power of* Elias? Which is plain that *John* the Baptiſt had his Commiſſion from *Elias*; for there was none greater in Heaven then *Elias* was at that time, for God was then on Earth, eating and drinking with Man as Man, as was before faid. Thus much may ferve to fatisfy all fober Men, who will not violently oppofe plain Scripture.

Again, you further object againſt that Saying of theirs, where they affirm, *That no one ever did declare the Knowledge of the true God, in his* Form *and* Nature, *as they have done.*

Now, in Anſwer to this, fay you, *There was* Sabulus *and* Noetus *held but one Perfon in the Diety, called by different Names*: Thefe, you Reprefentor call *Broachers of our Doctrin*, which you judg fo mifchevious.

CHAP. XII.

ANSWER.

IF thefe Bifhops of *Sabulus* and *Noetus* taught fo, they were in the right of it, and they might hint at Truth, but they wanted a full Revelation; for it was not Revealed to them as it is now, and thefe Two Prophets never read any of their Writings, neither do I think that there is any of them, that are truly theirs, in being: We have the Prophets and
Apoſtles

Apoftles Writings through Providence, to fhew that Chrift was the only God, altho they were very fparing in their Proof how God became Flefh, to what this Commiffion doth, and wherefore; why, becaufe the Miftery of God was not to be finifhed (according to *John*) until the Days of the Voice of the Seventh *Anty-Angel's* founding of his Trumpet, or Miniftry; Revel. 10. 7. namely the *Quakers*: And *Sabalus* and *Noetus* were before the founding of the Firft *Anty-Angel*, the *Papift* with Power.

Sabalus the Bifhop being about Two hundred Years after Chrift, and *Noetus* was Contemporary, with him; fo that this being in the time of the Ten Perfecutions, there was Truth then in the World, and a Trinity of Perfons in one Godhead had not got Footing at that time during the Ten Perfecutions.

But after *Religion* was fet up by Emperial Power, then *Bifhops* were chofen out of Learned and Philofophical Men, and Churches (as they called them) builded, and Riches given for their Support; then were *Sinods* and *Counfels* called, to eftablifh Error and formal Worfhip, and to fupprefs Truth: That was ever without outward Pomp and Glory.

Thus was *Noetus* and *Sabalus's* Doctrin Judged Herefy, both by *Trenitarian* and *Arian*; and tho they *Curfed*, *Excommunicated*, and *Condemned* each other, by feveral *Counfels*, *as if Hell was broke loofe*; and fo it was for the Thoufand Years time after *Satan's* Binding was ended, as foon as the Ten Perfecutions Revel. 20. were over, for then the Devil went forth to deceive the World with falfe Worfhip, as *John* declareth.

The *Arian*, being but as a Branch fprouted out of the *Roman Catholick*, altho in *Conftanfius's* Days, and fome time after a very great Branch, infomuch that the

the _Catholicks_ could not then boſt of Number; for
in the Counſel of _Ariminum_ and _Selencia_ there was
560 _Biſhops_, the greateſt Convention that ever was
known, and yet they Decreed the _Arian_ Faith: So
that will you _Catholicks_ ſay, _That Number is an Argument of Truth._

But whichſoever of them that got the Emperor óf
their ſide gained Power over the other ; ſo that both
of them, altho they perſecuted each other with deadly Hatred, as they got upermoſt in Power, never-
theleſs they could agree together, to kill. Chriſt in
his Members, and to tread the Holy City under Foot,
of innocent minded Men and Women, by their Pe-
nal Laws, that could not bow down to their outward Formalities and _Antichriſtian_ Principles : Theſe
were as Two Thieves that Trtuth was Cruſified between.

Now theſe _Catholicks_ prevailing, and they having,
not only the Scriptures order'd by the Emperor _Con-
ſtantine_ to be Tranſlated into their Tongue, but likewiſe their learned Counſels collected and gathered
into a Heap, and all the other Writings of preceding
Biſhops: Then muſt them Books and Traditional
Reports be viewed by the Learned, now made Biſhops, and what Agreed and Aquieſt with their
Principles was counted Apoſtolical ; and what did
not agree, was rejected and counted Hereſy ; or elſe
they Tranſlated them falſly, playcing down ſome
things of their Sayings, and leaving others out that
made againſt them.

And when any Man was by theſe eſtabliſhed Biſhops Judged or Accuſed for Hereſy, tho he lived before their Days, then all his Books muſt either be
Currupted or Burn'd; for they muſt be made to ſpeak
quite

Revel. 11. 1.

Matt. 27. 38.

Revel. 2. 2.

quite contrary to what they did in feveral things, on purpofe to make thofe Authors the more Contemptible: For it was ever fo, that all that are Non-Commiffionated Minifters of God, and fuch as head an Anty-Church, are for hideing Truth from the People, as the *Papifts* do the Scriptures, to the end they may keep up their flefhly Honour ; fo that there is but little known and received in the World at this Day, as well as heretofore, but the univerfal common Opinion.

Therefore it is, that your National and Traditional Churches doth fo found forth their own Triumphs, raife heaps of Authors of the *Firft Centuries,* as agreeing with their *Catholick Principles*; Crying *Antiquity, Church-Vifability, famous Men are on our Side,* &c.

When as the Truth on't is, all is but Clamour and Noife; for many of your Authors are meer Forgeries and Lies.

For Inftance.

1. There be feveral Books that have the Name of fuch Mens Works, as were never their Works; as *Abdyus* Bifhop of *Babilon,* is faid by fome of your Catalogue Makers to live in the Days of *Chrift*; others fay that he knew their great Church-Hiftorian *Egifipus,* that lived near Two Hundred Years after: Now the one of thefe muft be a Ly; and they make the Subftance of this Book to be of curious Talk with *Bodilis* or *Infernal Devils,* which is a mear *Roman Forgery.*

2. There is alfo that which is called Saint *James* the Apoftles Leturgie, which hath a Prayer in it for all that live in Monaftries, and yet there was none built of fome Hundreds of Years after the Apoftles Days.   3. And

3. And that *Egisipus*, before spoken of, hath Five Books under his Name : But it is said by some of your Church Writers, that *Ambrose* that *Roman-Church-Bishop* (who lived in the Year 380.) was not only the Traslator, but the Author of them Books ; which is like enough, for he was not chosen Bishop for his Goodness, but for his Greatness ; even as one of the Dukes of *Savoy* was chosen Pope for his Greatness sake, as your Church History doth shew.

4. These Corruptions have been very Common, and very Antient ; for *Dionisius* Bishop of *Corinth*, who lived about the Year of Christ Two Hundred, complained sadly of his being abused in this Nature : Therefore, said he, in one of his Books (if that Book was his) *I wrote several Epistles, but the Messengers of Satan hath sown them with Tares , pulling away some things, and puting to other some, for whom* (said he) *Condemnation is laid up.*

And as there was these Forgeries and Corruptions aforesaid, so likewise there is many of your other great Authors which you would make Apostolical, and yet they do not agree with you in several things that you quote them for ; nay some Differences are so great between you, that I wonder you do not Condemn them for Hereticks, as for Example.

1. *Turtulyon*, who lived in the time of the *Ten Persecutions*, being a great Historian, and by your Church counted famous, did not much contend for Bishops, nor much valued Ordination ; but said, *That Laymen were Priests*, and gave this Reason for it ; saying, *That after Faith is Received, then Man lives by his Faith, and that Faith*, said he, *becomes Christ's Vicar ; and from hence he concluded that Three Believers will make a Church.*

He

He alfo denyed *Childrens Baptifme*; and therefore, faid he, *Why haftneth this Innocent Age to the Remiffion of Sins, we are much more wary in worldly Things*; *Is it meet we fhould commit the Sacrament of Baptifme, which is a divine Thing, unto them we would not commit the Things of this Earth* : He alfo condemned Second Marriages, and much more Perfecution for Confience: All thefe things are quite contrary to you.

2. *Irinius*, Bifhop of *Lyons*, who, it is faid, knew *Ignafius* and *Policarbus*, yet he held and tought, the Souls Mortality.

3, And *Juftinus*, who lived in thofe Days, you cannot deny but that he did both hold and teach, *That God was in the Form of a Man from all Eternity.*

4. And further, There was never a one of all thefe aforefaid, that held a Trinity of Perfons in one God-Head; No not *Oregen* himfelf, whom your Church doth fo extol, altho he turned Apoftate, and denyed the Faith,and Sacrififed to Devils,to fave his Life; but what is he fo cry'd up, both by Papift and Proteftant, for; is it not for his lofty Stile, and philofophical Notions, and in that he would make his Divinity to ftoop unto his Philofophy ? For he held with *Plato*, 1. *The Souls Infufion, and tought that all Souls were made together, and fent down from Heaven to be Imbodyed.* 2. He Tought, *That after we rife again, we fhall have all need of Baptifme to purge us clean.* 3ly. *He in one place condemned Second Marriages, and in another Contradicts it again.* 4ly. *He Tought, that Devils were Bodilis-Spirits; and alfo, that all Devils would be faved at laft.* Thfs fure is it that pleafes you at a Haire.

But as to his Doctrin concerning God, that cannot pleafe you fo well, for the *Arians* challing him to be for them, and therefore they fay; That *Oregen* denyed *That the Son was to be Adored or Prayed too* ; *for he is,* faith *Oregen, not the Author, but the Procurer of the good Things of God :* So that we pray not to him, but to God for his fake. And *Augustin* your Saint produces this as *Oregen's* Opinion concerning God. And thus much as to your great Apoftolical Fathers, as you call them, who lived in the time of the Tén Perfecutions.

As to thofe other *Antient Popes, Bifhops, Fathers,* and *Counfels,* that have been fet up by the *Roman Imperial Power* and *Authority,* I fhall not treat on them here; for he that hath but a Grain of *fpiritual Senfe* predominating in him, will eafily fee them no other but the *Mother* of *Harlots,* or *Miftery Babilon,* that fets upon *Tongues, Nofions,* and *Languages,* as hath been unfolded in a Treacife intituled, *The White Devil uncafed;* which may come to be extant in time.

This is the Sum of your *Church-Hiftory ;* fo that what Satisfaction can any Man have by all your *Authors* and *Apoftolical Fathers,* as you call them, as alfo your *Tranflators* of their Works, who were moft of them *Corrupters,* each one endeavouring to force the Matter to fute with his own Opinions, as *Epephanius, Rufenus,* and feveral others, who it is faid corrupted feveral Authors.

So that all their Books are but troubled Waters to drink, being not of that Ephecafy as to quench the Thirft of Sin ; *for their* Silver *is become* Drofs, *their* Ifaiah 1. 22. John 4. 14. Wine *is mix'd with* Water *of a ftanding Poole.* This will not pafs currant with us, for no VVine to us like the VVine of the Spirit ; no VVater to us but the VVater of Life ; no Balme for us but what is in *Gilliad,* in one *Perfonal-God-Man, Chrift Jefus,* bleffed for ever, that will be accepted of with us, the
only

only true Chriftians in the World at this Day.

Therefore take you all your Books and Learning to yourfelves; we have but Three to Read, to wit, *the Prophets, the Apoftles, and the Witneffes of the Spirit:* In thefe is fulnefs of Perfection; for the Light and Life of their Words, fhining in our Hearts, is the *Rule, Prop, Stay,* and *Guide* of our *Faith* ; which is but one, and this one Faith hath one God of a fingle Perfon or Subftance for its Object to pitch it felf upon, and not a Trinity of Perfons, or Subftance; but *Father, Son* and *Holyghoft* is one fingle Subftance, and no more; which cannot be denyed, neither by Scripture, or fober Reafon ; for,

Firft, *Was not the Eternal* God-Head-Spirit *the everlafting Father.*

Secondly, *Was not that* glorious Body, *wherein God the Father did eternally Dwell,* The eternal Son.

Thirdly, *And was not that powerful Word, which proceeded from his God-Head-Spirit through his glorious Mouth the Holyghoft, or holy Spirit, by which he made the Worlds, and governeth all things.*

Is not this *Trinity* in *Unity,* and *Unity* in *Trinity,* more agreeable to the Scripture of Truth, then any other *Trinity,* to all Men that acknowledge but one eternal Being, and no more? Now your *Trinity of Perfons,* will neither be made to agree with Scripture Reafon nor Sence; fo that your ftriving to explain it doth but the more darken the Sence about your Airy God, and you are quite loft in your Definition, and now of late more than ever : Are you made a confounded *Babel,* and your Clargie doth clafh one againft another, which doth make your Hearers begin to ftager, as well it may : For,

Heb. 1. 3.
John 1. 13.
Ephef. 4. 5.
Ifa. 45. 21, 22.
Chap. 3. 10.

1*ſt.* One Party of your Church do th Hold and Teach, that God is [*Three diſtinƈt Perſons, and but one Subſtance*] which is a Contradiction.

2*ly.* The other Party of your Church Teacheth, That God hath not only [*Three diſtinƈt Perſons*] but [*Three diſtinƈt Subſtances likewiſe;*] and from hence doth boldly charge the *Homanſion,* or one Subſtance? with the Hereſy of S*abiliſm,* as they call it.

3*dly.* The contrary Party makes their Rejoynder again, and chargeth the other Party with holding of a plurality of Gods: For, ſay they, if there be [*Three Subſtances*] then there is [*Three Gods,*] which is true enough.

4*thly.* Again the adverſe Party Replys, ſaying, That if there be [*Three Perſons*] there muſt be [*Three Subſtances*] (which is true enough too:) And they give the Reaſon why they are to hold *Three Subſtances,* as well as *Three Perſons;* it being a forſt-put. For, ſay they, *there is now a greater Neceſſity than ever there was, to Hold and Maintain* Three *diſtinƈt* Subſtances, *as well as* Three Perſons: *Otherwiſe,* ſay they, *we are in great Danger to looſe the* Catholick Faith, *by the revival of the Hereſie of* Sabalus, *which walks publickly abroad, tho under the Diſguiſe of a new Name:* And therefore if we do not allow the God-Head intirely to be [Three diſtinƈt Subſtances] *as well as* [Three diſtinƈt Perſons] *then comes in* Sabaliſm : *And there's an end then* (ſay they) *of the Trinity.*

5*thly.* To this, the other old dark Light Replies, ſaying, *That if by Retaining the old Words of* [Three Perſons and one Subſtance] *there is Danger of looſing the* Catholick Faith, *it muſt be loſt out of the* Catholick Church : *And the Revolt by* Sabaliſm (ſay they) *muſt be both the moſt laſting, and the moſt general Apoſtatiſe*

that

that ever was foretold, or feared, should happen to the
Chriftian World. *But,* fay they, *we hope wee need
not to be frighted out of our Religion.*

And thus, you fee what a Confufion is fallen up-
on you; your *Babilon* is now crying out, *Alas, Alas!* Revel. 18. 10.
Did not the Prophets and Apoftles fpeak of thefe Things:
Now is fulfilled that Saying of *David's* to the full,
Divide their Tongues, O Lord, for I have feen Violence Pfal. 55. 9.
in the City.

Doth not this your Divifion tend to Confufion, Ifa. 11.11,15.
or is it not Confufion it felf in a fuperlative Degree?
For tho you be divided, yet our God is not divided, 1 John 5, 7.
but is one, Yefterday, to Day, and for ever: For 20.
I demand,-

Firft, How can Chrift be called *the greate, the* Heb. 13. 8.
High and Mighty God, if he hath Two other Gods to Titus 2. 13.
fhare with him? And, 1 Tim. 1. 17. & 6.12..

Secondly, How can Chrift be *Eternal* in your *Creed,*
if he were begotten?

Thirdly, And how can that, which receives a Being
from another, ever be made equal with that which
hath its being of it felf alone?

Certainly, whatever you *Trinitarians* fay to the
contrary, yet it is evident that you make Chrift no
more than a titular God, the very fame with *John
Biddle,* that you fo much difown in your Pamphlet:
But I cannot fee any great Difference between you;I am
fure you are as much out of the Way of Truth as he.

For, faid *John Bidle,* *Chrift is our Lord and God:*
But how, *Why,* faid he, *not Really, but Apelitive, as
Magiftrates are called Gods;* and fo he makes him
God by Deputation, as to Title; being God, not in
Nature, but in Name; and fo is fubordinate to
God.

Now

Now, do not you do fo too; for you make the Son but to be begotten : And if you will make him God, yet he muſt be divided from the Father and Holyghoſt. Now this is certain, that if there be a Father diſtinct from that bleſſed Body of Chriſt, it muſt then be as *John Bidle* ſaid; and therefore it is, that *John Bidle*, as well as *Arius* and *Seſinus*, make him but Man; becauſe they would have but one ſingle God : But you, if you make him God, yet you will divide him from the Father, and from the Holyghoſt; and fo, at the beſt, you make him but a Third part God.

And whereas you are fo bold, as to condemn *Sabulus* and *Noetus*, for worſhiping one perſonal God, under the Names of *Father, Son*, and *Holyghoſt*; condemning and judging them for Broachers of Hereſy, how will you free yourſelves from this Crime: As alſo thoſe Counſels of *Arians* and *Trenitarians*, as curſed them and their Principles; together with thoſe Counſels and Sinods, on both ſides judging and condemning each other with deadly Malice, as your Church Hiſtory doth ſhew: What, were thoſe the Church of God ? No.

But when God gathers up his Jewels, many of _{Mal.3. 15. 16.} thoſe that have been judged Hereticks will riſe Saints, _{17, 18.} and many of thoſe that your Churches have Canonized for Saints, will riſe Devils : For no Perſecutors of Conſcience will eſcape the Stroke. If any Man object *Paul*'s perſecuting the Church, they may know that *Paul* at that time acknowledged no Jeſus at all; therefore when both ſides acknowledges a Jeſus, take heed how you Perſecute.

I have been ſomthing larger than I intended, as to the Church-Hiſtory, and that becauſe your Church doth

doth fo much boaft and Glory upon Antiquity, like the Papifts; for there is no great Difference between you nor the other Churches, only in outward things; for the effential Points of Faith is one and the fame with you all; for you have all one God, and one Devil, one Heaven and one Hell. So that if one of you be true, you are all true; and if one of you be falfe, ye are all falfe: Therefore it were well, if your Reafon would be fo moderate, as to bear with, and forbear one another; being you are all one, both in the Root, and in the Fruit, but that you will never do; but on the contrary, you will ever be exciting the Magiftrates to Perfecution and Bloodfhed: But Revel. 17. 3. happy is it for that Nation in the Temporal, and that & 15. 6. 18. & Nation or Holy City in the Spiritual, whofe Magi- 18. 24. ftrates are fo prudent, as not to harken to the Priefts Inftigations; but on the contrary, to ftop the Courfe of the Violent by wholfom Laws.

Thefe are thofe good Beafts, or head Magiftrates, Revel. 4. 6. fpoken of by the Scriptures, who are faid to have *Eyes before and behind:* The Eye of Faith before, which fhews them that Confcience belongs to God ; and the Eye of Reafon behind, to fee that all Affairs in the Temporal be kept well, exercifing Juftice and true Judgment; preferving and defending the Innocent Rom. 13. 3. who break not the Civil Law: And on the other hand, punifhing the Tranfgreffors of any of the Ci- Acts 5. 38. vil Laws of the Land, according to their Demerit.

Thefe, and fuch like Magiftrates, are the truly Nurfing Fathers, and fhall profper : *This we leave to Providence, and proceed.*

In the latter end of your Pamphlet, you pretend a great many of Contradictions committed by *Lodowick Muggleton* and *John Reeve*; but the Anfwer before
might

might ferve for them all that are worth the Anfwering; yet I fhall Anfwer to Two or Three Things more that you charge againft them.

In Page 25. You fay, *That* John Reeve *doth affirm, that no Man can foretel Eclipfes of the* Sun *and* Moon, *but by Revelation: From whence,* fay you, *the Aftrologers are much beholding to him, who tells them they write their Alminacks by Revelation, if they therein foretel Eclipfes, as what Aftrologer doth not.*

CHAP. XIII.

ANSWER.

1. **H**ERE you wreft their Words, and frame a wrong Senfe of them; for the Time when an Eclipfe falls out is one thing, and the Time of the Ephects of Working is another: Of fome of the Eclipfes, the Aftrologers fay, the Time of their Ephects laft for fo many Months, others the Time of fo many Years, before the Ephects will have done working.

Wherefore then it follows, that *John Reeve* doth not fay, That none of the Figurative Marchants doth know when, or at what time an Eclipfe will fall, but their Ephects, and time of them Ephects, how long they will be in working: *Thefe Things,* faid *John Reeve, can no Man know, but by Infpiration;* which is pofitively True.

And thus you, Church-Doctor, raife Slanders to blaft their Reputation; and fo Truth comes to be vilified,

lified as I fhewed before, for Truth may be buried under Falfehood for a time.

Again, *pag.* 25, you charge them with another Error, faying, That *they affirm that the Eclipfe of the Moon is never but when it is near the Sun:* When as, fay you, it is manifeft that its Eclipfe is when it is oppofite to the Sun, and that the Earth is between them, which doth occafion it by with-holding its borrowed Light. But to this I anfwer.

2. Here again you haye abufed *John Reeve,* and in plain terms bely'd him; which one would think a Man of that feeming Purity would not have done: For *John Reeve* doth not deny its Eclips when oppofite to the Sun; but faith (for thefe are his Words) the Eclipfe of the Moon is through her near conjunction with the Natural Light or Ruler of the Day, or a Planatary Fire, anfwerable to its nature that occafions the Eclipfe.

Now this we do affirm, and your Aftrologers do not deny it but that there are Stars of a fiery nature, and Experience fhews it: For what is the reafon that there is more heat when the Sun is in *Leo,* then there is when it enters *Cancer,* when as the *Sun* is neareft to us, when it enters that Sign, but only that the Heat is occafioned by the rifing of fome Fiery Stars, as that which they call the Dogg Star, and others of the like nature.

So likewife the occafion of the Moons Eclipfe, it is not by the Sons not rendring its borrowed Light, by reafon of the Earths interpofing her felf betwixt thofe Lumenaries; but it is through her being near to fome of them Fiery Stars, as thofe which the Aftrologers call the *Dragons-Head,* or *Dragons-Tail;* one of which being always near to the Moon when fhe fuffers an Eclipfe. K 3. We

3. We do likewife affirm that the Moon borrows no Light from the Sun, but that it is a real created Light of it felf; for *Mofes* faith, That *God made two great Lights*; but your *Aftrologers* and you fay, That God made but one : Whether fhould we believe, *Mofes* or you ? for faith *Mofes*, *One of them is made to rule the Day, and the other is made to rule the Night.* •

4*ly.* The Sun and Moon are of contrary natures, one is fiery hot, the other is cold and watery ; therefore it is contrary to Reafon that the one fhould receive any Light from the other, and therefore there can be no agreement betwixt them, for Experience fhews us that the Moon is cold and watery, being made out of the Water, and fo is the Lady of the Water, and occafions the Ebbing and Flowing of the Seas, and the running of all Rivers, drawing the Waters after her, as the Loadftone doth Iron.

But on the other Hand, the Sun is hot and firy, being the Captain of all Fire, and fo draws combuftible Matter up to it felf, which occafioneth Thunder, which is a War betwixt Fire and Water ; and thus they appear in their contrariety of Natures, which we fee further by Experience, that the clearer that the Sun doth fhine, the hotter it is; but the clearer the Moon doth fhine, the colder it is.   ·

So that from what is faid, may be feen who the Aftrologers are moft beholding to, whither to you, or *John Reeve*, let all Men judg; for *John Reeve*, in this Prinfiple, is as contrary to the Aftrologers, as the Sun and Moon are contrary in Nature.

Furthermore, You object againft *John Reeve*, for faying that the Sun, Moon, and Stars move all in one *Firmament*: And for faying, *That they are not much bigger then they appear to us.* To this you fay,

That

That they are quite contrary, and that they move in feve-
ral Orbes, and that each Orbe at fo much diftance from
each other, as the Aftroligers affirm.

C H A P. XIV.

A N S W E R.

1. **I**S it not as good Senfe, and better, to believe,
That the Sun, Moon, and Stars move all in one
Firmament, or Heaven, as fo many as Nine feveral Hea-
vens, as your blind Aftrologers teach you : And yet our
flefhly Eyes can pierce through them all ; neverthelefs every one of thefe muft be fo many Thoufands
of Miles beyond each other ; and this blind Opinion
muft be ratified forfooth, becaufe the Planets and
fixed Stars have feveral Motions ; and therefore from
hence you will have thefe feveral Heavens, and thefe
their differences in Motion, muft fhew their difference in Hight and Subftance.

2. Becaufe *Saturn* moves fo floly, as to be near upon Thirty Years in finifhing his Courfe through the
Twelve Signs, whereas the *Sun* finifhes his in one
Year: Therefore, from hence, do you conclude, that
he muft be of neceffity Thirty times higher, and
Thirty times bigger than the Sun, and Thirty times
further to go ; nay, and the next Orbe above *Saturn*
to move fo flow, as to be Forty Thoufand Years in
finifhing his Courfe: Pray how many Millions of
Miles is it to that Heaven, or *Primum Mobila?* One
of your Mathematifians fay it is,*One hundred and feventy*
Millions eight hundred and three Miles. K 2 Is

Is this your Wifdom, in which you fay weare not capable to anfwer you in? I pray, Is this good Pulpit Doctrin? One of your Minifters that I did know, whofe Name was *Mountney*, did mount fo high, as to affirm, in the Pulpit, to his Parifhioners, that it was fo far to the *primum Mobil.t, That if it were poffible to fling a Millftone down from thence, that it would, be Seven Tears before it would reach this Earth:* And yet in another Doctrin he taught, *That a departed Soul would be in Heaven in a Moment,* which is much higher than that *primum Mobila.*

And your reverend Doctor *More,* before quoted, muft be remembred here, for he Taught, *That a Star of the firft Magnitude is Twenty thoufand times biger than this Earth, and Nine hundred thoufand times biger than the Moon.*

Thefe are your rare learned Men, I wonder how they could get a Line of that length to meafure fo far, and yet to ftand upon this Earth: But let them go on, for the time of their Sopheftry is almoft at an end. But to conclude this Point; as you upon our Principles of the Sun, Moon, and Stars aforefaid, do call all Men to be Judges againft us; fo we, to retort your Language, do call all fober Men to judge, whether your Opinion of Sun, Moon, and Stars be not an Error of the greateft Magnitude; and alfo, whether you have done us Juftice, yea or nay. *And fo much in anfwer to your firft Query.*

Chap.

C H A P. XV.

SIR, your Second Query, or latter part of your
Pamphlet, was to prove *Lodowick Muggleton* falfe
from his Interpretation of the 11*th. Chapter* of the
Revelation of *John*.

But your Proof is but your Denyal, for you do
not fo much as fhew the meaning of one Word in all
that Chapter: If they could but aflended up to Heaven
in a Cloud, as they had fhewed how *Mofes* and *Jefus*
did, all had been well enough; even as the *Jews*, if
they could but have feen *Elias* to have come in Perfon, as *John Baptift* did, then they would have believed as they faid.

So, if you could but have feen thefe Prophets to
aflend up in a Cloud, then perhaps you would have
faid you would have believed them : *But foft* (fay you)
*they are not the Two Witneffes, for they cannot aflend to
Heaven, for John Reeve* is dead: *Befides* (fay you)
*they muft have been put to Death by the Hands of Violence,
and then to have rifen again, and afcended to Heaven, in
the fight of all Men.*

This is all the Interpretation you can give of them,
which is none at all, and all the Proof you have a-
gainft them : And as to *Lodowick Muggleton's* Interpretation of that Chapter, you feem to be at a great
Lofs about it, being aftonifhed at his Words : *For,*
(fay you) *I cannot tell how to reconcile his Words*; and
from hence you fling all off to others, faying, *Reconcile them as can, for I cannot.*

Two

And what is the Difference and Matter that cannot be Reconciled : *Why*, fay you, *he faith, That they Two are the Two Witneffes* ; and yet they fay, *That the Body of thofe Two Witnefles are the Letter of the Scriptures, and that the Witneffes, or Letter, was flain* 1350 *Years before, and yet was flain in them again by the Beaft out of the bottomlefs Pit.* To this I anfwer.

1*ft.* Here you would have the Letter to be flain, whenas it was the Spirit and Life of that Letter that was flain ; for the Life being gone, therefore the Letter of the Scripture remained as a dead Body, in regard there was none living that could give a true Interpretation of it.

Now this Spirit and Life was killed 1350 Years ago ; for the laft of the Ten Perfecutions did kill and root out all the true ordained Bifhops, or Minifters of the Gofpel ; fo that there was none left to give the *Holyghoft* to others, by laying on of Hands ; fo then there was no quickening Power remaining until a new Commiffion was given, which now is fulfilled at this Day ; for the fame Spirit that gave the other Witneffes their Commiffion, hath chofe thefe to be Witneffes.

3*dly.* So that they having received that fame Spirit of Life from God, as the others had ; therefore it is they only that can, and do Interpret the Letter of the Scripture ; for the Scripture is put into their Hands, as the Priefthood was into the Hands of *Aaron*, and they by their Interpretation do put Life into the Scriptures, making it to ftand upon its Feet in the Confciences of Men and Women, with great Power, both to the Seed of Faith, and to the Seed of Reafon, to fave and deftroy ; for Words of Truth have Spirit and Life.

4*thly.*

4*thly.* And as that Spirit of Reafon did kill that Spirit of Life that did fpeak that Letter, fo that now that Spirit and Life is come into them again, they will ftand upon their Feet, and kill the Spirit of Reafon with a Death Eternal; for there is now both Body and Life in the Scriptures, and it is the Body of the Witneffes of the Spirit, which is not a dead Body, but a living Body now, and fo will remain to the end of the World.

5*thly.* Again, whereas you do affirm, *That thefe Witneffes do declare, that the Spirit and Life was killed in them by the Beaft out of the Bottomlefs Pit, in their Perfecutors :* That faying of yours is utterly falfe, and you did it malitioufly, on purpofe that his Words might not be reconciled ; for *Lodowick Muggleton* did fay, *That the Beaft out of the Bottomlefs Pit made War againft them, and would have killed them, if their Law could have done it.* And that roaring Lyon *Jefferies* did fay afterwards, *That he was forry that their Laws were fo unprovided, that they could not take away* Muggleton'*s Life.*

So that it is apparent, that the Spirit and Life of thefe Two Witneffes is not killed; but after the Two Witneffes of the Spirit are dead, the Spirit and Life will remain in vigour.

6*thly.* Wherefore as the other Two Witneffes of *Water* and *Blood* did laft to the end of the appointed time of their Commiffions, even fo likewife will the Revelation of this Commiffion laft to the end of the World ; for tho the Doctrin is declared as to the Subftance ; yet in that Doctrin will Revelation atife, grow and increafe, in fuch as hear it and underftand it, to their eternal Happinefs, Joy, and Glory; and fhall Prevail and Triumph over all Forms and Opinions

nions in Religion, that now totters more than ever
through its own Inſtability.

And now Sir, are you not either Blind or Malitious, or both, that would forge Contradictions where
there is none; yea, and to make Lies, on purpoſe to
make Truth appear Infamous? So that are not you a
Shifter of all Shifters, and know not where to fix,
or what to ſay, or how to diſprove it, either by
Scripture or ſober Reaſon? It's a poor Shift to falſi-
fy the Words of your Oponant, becauſe you have
not anything that ſeems plauſible to Anſwer.

Sir, is this your Learning? Pray do you believe
that Book of the Revelation by St. *John*, to be true
Revelation, and a part of holy Writ? If you ſay
you do, then why will you not give your own Cen-
timents of ſo much as one Verſe, and tell the Meaning thereof? And if this Interpretation of theirs be
not good Senſe, why do you not Reprove them with
better?

But finding your Ignorance to be ſuch, therefore
it had been better for you to have let this Book alone,
and plainly to have ſaid, *That it was Sealed, and you
could not read it in its own Senſe.* And it had been
better for you to have let theſe Two Witneſſes alone,
and all the Believers of it alone; but you were appointed to that end, that your Lies and Slandees a-
gainſt it may bring you to a full Reward.

For this Book of the Revelation by *John* was not
writen for your Edification, but for the Inſtruction
of this laſt Witneſs, and Benifit of the Seed of Faith,
to the End of the World, as a peculiar Bleſſing Seal'd
to them from Heaven: And therefore by this Bleſſing of Faith and Knowledge in the Scriptures of
Truth, which is now given unto us, we do from
hence

hence that you have no part of the Bleſſing of this Book of the *Revelation* of St. *John*, as may appear by theſe Seven Particulars following.

As *Firſt*, This Commiſſion of the Spirit hath ſeen into the Book of Life, wherein they have found the Names of the Prophets, Apoſtles, and the Witneſſes of ⁽Chap 20. 15.⁾ the Spirit Recorded there, as true Commiſſionated Meſſengers of God; but your Name was not found there as a Miniſter of God: *This is the firſt Evidence of your Excluſion.*

Secondly, Theſe Witneſſes, and the Believers there-of, have looked and ſeen thoſe *Hundred forty and four* ⁽Cha. 14. 3.⁾ *thouſand Virgins that were Redeemed from the Earth, ſtanding with the Lamb, their only God, on Mount* Sion, *ſinging that new Song of, all Praiſe to the Lamb*: But you, not having learn'd that Song of, *all Praiſe to the Lamb*, were not found amongſt them; but we, look-⁽Ca. 17. 5.⁾ ing about, have ſeen you in that great City, *Miſtery* ⁽& 22. 18.⁾ *Babilon*, the Mother of all Harloting and Blaſphem-ing Prieſts; who are ſaid, by the Spirit, to have the Curſe of this Book, for ading and taking away from it. For you add your own Imaginations to it, and ſo from thence will make your own confounded Rea-ſon to be the Judg of it; as I ſhew'd before in *Chap* 2.

Thirdly, As we have ſeen you add your own vain Thoughts to it, ſo likewiſe have we ſeen you taking away from the Words of this Propheſy, and the ⁽Chap. 11. 2.⁾ Two Witneſſes thereof: For you will not ſuffer thoſe laſt true Prophets to have any Footing here, but would thruſt them out of the Book of Life, and ⁽Chap. 18. 7.⁾ thruſt yourſelf into it.

But this Commiſſion ſheweth us, That God will take away your part out of the Book of Life; not that you had any there, but that you thought you had.

L

had, and thought your Name was there, but you
are not in the Book of Life to be found, neither as
a Teacher, nor as a true Believer, as thofe Two Witneſſes are and the true Believers thereof: We have
found our Names in this Book of Life of the Lamb,
the only and alone wife God, to our eternal Comfort, and his everlafting Praife.

Forthly, Again, you have further taken away from
this Book, in that you denyed God to have any Body, Face, or Shape: So that as the Bleſſing of this
Book is, *That the Saints ſhall ſee his Face*; fo the
Curfe of this Book is, *That ſuch as have denyed him*, as
aforefaid, *ſhall never ſee his Face to their Comfort.*

Fifthly, you have likewife taken away from this
Book, in that you teach, that the *Alpha* and *Omega*
did not die: But this Book doth declare that the
Alpha and *Omega*, the Firſt and the laſt did die, and
ſhed his Blood; by which he redeemed his Elect Seed;
fo what part can you have in this Purchafe, feeing
you deny that God had any Blood, or offered up any
Life by ſhedding of the fame.

Sixthly, You alfo further add, and take away from
this Book of *John*, in that you ſay, *That there is a God
diſtinct from Chriſt*: And further fay, *That Chriſt Jeſus our Lord is not the ſole God*: But this Book of
John owns no other God at all but Jefus Chriſt; giving him the Titles of *Firſt* and *Laſt*, the *Alpha* and
Omega, *King of Kings*, *God*, *very God*, *true God*, *great
and almighty God, and the God of all Prophets*: Where
then ſhould there be any other God befides Jefus
Chriſt our Lord; for this divine Apoſtle, who lived
and leaned in the Bofom of this Lord, knew not any
other God, as is abundantly proved.

Margin notes:
Chap. 3. 5.
Chap. 22. 4.
& 2. 18. & 19.
12. & 1. 16.
Chap. 1, 8. 18.
& 2. 8
1 John 5. 20.
Revel. 19. 16,
17. & 15. 13.
& 1. 8. & 22.
5. 16. & 18. 2.
& 15. 1.

Seventh-

Seventhly, and lastly, This God, the Lord Jesus, you have Renounced, his Prophets you have Perfecuted and Belied, the true Faith you have defpifed; for you have not only Contradicted and Difpifed the Doctrin of the Second Commiffion, which was the Commiffion of Blood, but you have alfo, to agrivate your Crime, called the Doctrin of this Third and Laft Commiffion, which is the Commiffion of the Spirit (and which is one of them three great Armies that in Heaven will follow the Lamb upon white Horfes, which is the Righteoufnefs of Faith in his blefled Perfon : I fay you have called this Commiffion) *Blafphemy, Delufion, Deceat : And that it is (* fay you) *made up of Impiety, Nonfenfe and Abfurdities :* And in general, calls them *mifchevious Principles, Confufion and Contradiction ; and that we are a pernici ous and contemptable Sect,* &c. `Chap. 19. 14.`

So that, from hence, it doth plainly appear, That you have brought yourfelf under the Judgment and Senfure of that Book of *John,* and of this Commiffion of the Spirit, which doth fo fully explain that *Prophefy,* being fent to finifh the *Miftery of God:* And now behold it is finifhed, and *you* have heard, and now *you* will find, that Power belongeth unto this God, and to this his Commiffion of the Spirit. `Chap. 19. 15. 20. & 21. 27.` `Chap. 10. 7.` `Pfal. 62. 11.`

F I N I S.

www.ingramcontent.com/pod-product-compliance
Lightning Source LLC
Chambersburg PA
CBHW030008030726
47499CB00008B/2946